ON AND ON

A NOVEL

Also by Eric von Schrader

The *Intersecting Worlds* Trilogy:

A Universe Less Traveled
A Universe Disrupted
A Universe Revealed

ON AND ON

A NOVEL

Eric von Schrader

ABSOM BOOKS

ISBN 979-8-9859304-9-8
Library of Congress Control Number: 2026904914

ABSOM Books
Carpinteria, CA

Dedicated to my dearest
Becky Brittain von Schrader.
Without her love and encouragement, none of my books
would exist.

CONTENTS

A Fresh Start

CHERYL RICARD NEEDED THIS JOB. She needed it bad. And she needed it now.

Anxiety twitched and crackled inside her head as she watched the man across the desk read her application. She tried to breathe slowly, like Dr. Pettus taught her years ago. In through the nose, out through the lips. The man, Paul Boland, glanced up at her, smiled politely, then went back to reading. Cheryl froze. *Did he hear me breathing? Have I already blown the interview?* An hour's worth of thoughts ripped through her mind in about five seconds.

Boland's desk is a disaster. Folders stacked in a chaotic pile, with paper corners sticking out. Tangled cables running from the laptop to the monitor. Coffee stains around the edge of his mug. I could so easily organize the pile and tap the stray papers back into place. Probably not a good idea to do it now, but if I get the job, I'll do it when he isn't here. I'll come in early and take care of his desk each morning before he arrives. He'll tell the other project managers that I'm the best associate project manager he's ever had. Maybe the best in the whole company. He'll nominate me for an award. Cousin Bob tells me that they love awards in this company. Everyone gets awards. Boland has a wall full of plaques and certificates. I know I'll only have a cubicle, not an office with a door, so there won't be much wall space. That's fine. I don't care about trivial stuff like that. My quiet efficiency will speak for me. Helping Paul—I'll work so hard he'll tell me to call him Paul—by taking care of the details, anticipating what he needs before he has to ask.

"You have a very diverse employment history, Ms. Ricard. Hospitality, animal rescue, childcare, among others. Why is that?"

"I enjoy solving problems and finding ways to help the organization be more efficient. I've learned a lot from every job I've had."

Paul nodded. Cheryl relaxed a bit. She had practiced this answer and it worked.

"What do you see as your strengths?"

Another easy one. "I'm thorough and detail oriented. I don't rest until the work is done and done right. Too many people are sloppy. I'm not one of them."

"I see. Getting details right is certainly important in our business."

Paul followed up by asking her about her last job, as the office manager for a plumbing contractor, but he was just going through the motions. He was desperate for help. His last two associate project managers had quit within the past six months. One couldn't handle the long hours that ruined too many evening and weekend plans; the other got fed up after a last-minute demand forced her to throw out days of work only hours before a big deadline. And Paul's busiest time of the year was right around the corner.

Cheryl's cousin Bob, who had set up this interview for her, told her that as long as she didn't screw it up, she would get the job. "Just keep your mouth under control. Think before you speak. He's in no position to be choosy." Bob's patronizing tone annoyed her, but she also was in no position to be choosy. Her credit cards were nearly maxed out and she was going to lose her apartment if she didn't come up with back rent soon. She had a recurring habit, which didn't appear on her resume, of pissing people off. Even when she was right about something, which she often was, she managed to go too far. After she got annoyed and started telling people where to stuff it, everything unraveled before she could control herself. This pattern had begun in high school, when the other kids realized how easy and fun it was to bait Cheryl, a shy, awkward nerd, into outbursts of impotent rage. After several of these episodes, the school counselor suggested to her parents that seeing a therapist might be helpful for Cheryl. They didn't like the insinuation that their daughter was "troubled" and no one in the family had ever seen a psychologist. Still, they agreed to send her to the therapist the counselor recommended. Cheryl hated this idea, but Dr. Pettus turned out to be a lifesaver. She actually listened to Cheryl and wasn't fazed by her fears and anxieties. She said it was all about managing your reactions. "People are going to act in ways you don't like. They'll be mean sometimes. You can't stop that. But you don't have to let it rule you." She taught Cheryl how to calm herself with slow, deep breathing. "Don't think about anything else for just a moment and take five breaths." Because of Dr. Pettus, Cheryl got through high school.

Paul Boland didn't know what to make of this quiet, plain young woman sitting across from him. With her dull brown hair cut sharp below the ears, brown eyes behind barely visible lashes and eyebrows, pale skin, and thin lips, she was the kind of person who would be easily overlooked in a crowded room. Her flat expression didn't reveal much personality, but he wasn't looking for personality. He needed someone who would show up and do the work—call vendors, keep tabs on other departments, manage spreadsheets, handle event logistics, and anything else that popped up. Every day, he was on a hamster wheel trying to keep up with the demands and questions that his boss, Jack Weatherly, constantly rained down on him. Weatherly brought millions of dollars of business into Success Dynamics—and never let anyone forget it—so he got whatever he wanted. From the moment Paul entered his office in the morning until Weatherly's last late-night voicemail, he was always behind.

Her employment history seemed a bit sketchy, a mishmash of jobs that didn't make a lot of sense, but Bob Ricard, whom Paul respected, vouched for her work ethic and intelligence. Most importantly, she had one major thing in her favor—she was available now. Paul reached across the desk to shake her hand. "Welcome to the SDI team, Cheryl."

"Thank you, Mr. Boland."

"Call me Paul."

"Thank you, Paul."

"Your orientation will begin first thing Monday morning."

From the parking lot, Cheryl phoned Bob to give him the good news. "Wonderful!" he said, "You have all the skills to be good at this job, and you can make some decent money. Keep your head down and focus on the work. And please remember one thing: People at SDI *never, ever* talk about anything remotely political. Don't get started on the environment, climate change, or any of that stuff. It will only cause you trouble."

Sellout

"NONE OF THESE OUTFITS ARE GOING TO CUT IT." Amy Westover shook her head as she looked through Cheryl's closet on Saturday morning.

"I wore them for my last job."

Amy laughed, "You were working with plumbers, remember? I don't know diddly about this new place, Success whatever, but I'm pretty sure their business has nothing to do with unclogging toilets. You have to look like you belong there."

Cheryl sighed. She had met Amy while volunteering at the Climate Crisis Coordinating Committee, known as C4, the environmental organization they were both passionate about. Amy was her best friend—and these days just about her only friend. She was smart about people in ways that Cheryl wasn't. "What do you want me to do?"

"We're going shopping! Today!"

"You know I can't on Saturday afternoon." Now Amy sighed. Cheryl's obsession with Saturday housecleaning was a quirk that Amy didn't understand, but had gotten used to.

"Okay. Tomorrow. I'll pick you up at noon."

"Are the thrift shops open on Sundays?"

"Forget thrift shops. We're going to the Galleria so you won't look like a Mormon wife."

"I hate that place! Those stores sell all that synthetic stuff, made by child labor in Bangladesh!"

"Tomorrow. Noon."

Cheryl was worn out after two hours roaming every women's clothing store in the Galleria mall to end up at H&M, which Amy now declared to be the best for what they needed. It wasn't easy to keep up with Amy's long-legged strides as she led the charge through the store, pulling item after item out of the racks for Cheryl to look at. Amy had definite theories on colors and accessorizing. "Mix and match strategically and you can have a fresh look every day. When we're done here, you'll be bulletproof—like Wonder Woman! No one at that company is going to have the nerve to give you any crap." Cheryl, who never thought about clothes, was bewildered, but Amy's enthusiasm and endless wisecracks made the experience kind of fun.

Now came the hard part. Cheryl laid a tall stack of clothes on the checkout counter. She was buying more in a single day than she usually did in a year. When she swiped her credit card, the last one that still hadn't hit its limit, she prayed it would be accepted. *Approved* appeared on the little screen. Cheryl wasn't sure whether to be relieved or depressed. *This is what selling out means. You run yourself deeper into debt so you can toil in the bowels of heartless corporations while they destroy the planet and line their pockets.*

Sellout. The word floated over Cheryl's head as she clipped the price tags off her new outfits and hung them in the closet. It perched on her shoulder as she sauteed vegetables in her tiny kitchen and mixed them with ramen noodles for dinner. While she ate, she pondered the events and choices that had led her away from her principles, one after another, to become a sad, pathetic sellout. *What am I doing wrong? Other people have lives that make sense. When they do something, it works—at least part of the time. Why can't I have that?* But everything Cheryl had ever done fell apart, sooner or later.

Because of her good grades in high school, Cheryl earned a modest scholarship, which allowed her to attend the University of Missouri in Columbia, a few hours away from her home in St. Louis. With the in-state tuition, a student job, and loans, Cheryl could get by. Her parents didn't have a lot of money for her education and believed that self-reliance would be good for her. Cheryl was excited about college—a chance to escape the catastrophe of high school and start over.

She majored in chemistry, an orderly and precise subject she loved. If you performed an experiment properly, the chemical reaction would turn out the way it was supposed to. There was no room for opinions, speculation, or debate. Cheryl felt at home with the periodic table, acids and bases, reagents, and catalysts. She kept her lab supplies and instruments clean and organized. Her class reports were logical and well-structured. Best of all, she could do most of the work by herself, alone in the lab. The chemistry building on campus became her safe, soothing little world. Her parents, neither of whom had gone to college, were pleased by her decision to major in chemistry. "Always plenty of jobs for chemists."

In February of senior year, she saw a flyer for a meeting of the college hiking club and, on a whim, decided to go. She watched a slide show about upcoming day hikes and weekend campouts. Afterwards, one student gave a short talk on hiking boots and camping gear at a table full of samples. Cheryl had never owned hiking boots, so she had a lot of questions. The student, who introduced himself as Todd Blasingame, was happy, actually eager, to answer them. "The shoes you have now may be fine for day hikes, if you wear thick socks. Come on the outing this Saturday. I'll be there and will make sure your shoes are comfortable."

Todd walked side by side with Cheryl the entire hike. He talked a lot, the kind of thing that usually made Cheryl nervous, but not this time. He was a "PoliSci" major. She wasn't sure what that was, but realized that it had to do with politics when he said, "I want to work in government."

"Like get elected?"

"Maybe someday. I'm mostly interested in policy. In figuring out what will actually make people's lives better."

He asked Cheryl what she was majoring in. When she said "chemistry," he smiled and raised his eyebrows. "So which oil company do you want to work for?"

"Huh? Why an oil company?"

"Isn't that what the chemistry department is all about? Keeping the oil companies and other big polluters well-staffed?"

Cheryl didn't know what to say…. "Uhm, that's not what I'm doing, I like chemistry. It's interesting."

"Hey, I'm not saying you're a polluter, but don't deny the system you're in."

"Aren't you part of the same system? Politics isn't that pure."

"I know what I'm dealing with. We shouldn't be blind to what's going on around us."

Todd and Cheryl went for pizza after that first hike. He both charmed her and challenged her with his ideas about power and the environment and everyone's responsibility to make the world a better place. She had never thought much about any of these issues.

A few days later, he invited her to his apartment to watch the Al Gore film, *An Inconvenient Truth*, about global warming, a topic she had barely paid attention to. Cheryl's eyes were forever opened. Nothing could ever be more important than the battle to save the environment. Todd laid out his dream of building a host of committed activists to move the public to demand change. That night, Cheryl imagined working side by side with him on this great mission. She vowed to never sell out, like the other chemistry majors were eagerly doing. She plunged into learning everything she could about climate change. She read books, watched online lectures by climate scientists, and downloaded technical reports from the Intergovernmental Panel on Climate Change. She stared in horror at the graphs of ever-increasing levels of heat-trapping gases in the atmosphere. *It's all chemistry!* She was astounded that people weren't up in arms to demand a stop to the madness. "That's why we need politics," Todd said as he inhaled from a joint one night, "It's the only way to mobilize people to solve the problems of society."

The next month, she went with Todd to a march on campus to demand that the university divest the fossil fuel stocks in its portfolio. A large photo on the front page of the student newspaper showed Cheryl shouting angrily as she held up a sign that read *Get oil out of our education NOW!* It caused quite a stir in the chemistry department, which, as Todd said, valued its relationships with the major petroleum companies. Though Cheryl was one of the department's best students, the job interviews her professors were lining up for her were scrubbed.

By then Cheryl didn't care. She had thrown herself into the environmental cause—and the arms of Todd Blasingame.

No boy had ever paid so much attention to her, and she fell hard for him. He enjoyed the adulation in her eyes and saw her as a naive science nerd whose consciousness he could raise—and also a very pleasant bed companion. She didn't realize she was only a supporting player in the epic drama of Todd Blasingame's climb to well-deserved prominence.

A turning point came one evening as he was holding forth in front of their friends, over pitchers of beer in a bar. He grandly declared that effective climate campaigns had to hammer home a simple message. "Carbon dioxide emissions cause global temperature increases. Period. Like ninety-nine percent." Cheryl pointed out that the actual figure was seventy-six percent, with methane and other gases making up the rest. From memory, she cited the source for the correct numbers. "And methane is worse because it persists in the atmosphere for years." Todd was wrong and Cheryl was right, of course. The friends were impressed, but Todd sulked the rest of the evening. That was the beginning of the end.

He broke up with her in a busy restaurant, without warning, a few days before graduation. It was the shortest conversation they ever had. For once, he was tongue-tied. He stood up and left before she knew what had hit her. Then, he didn't answer her frantic calls, texts, and emails. She went to his apartment, but he had moved out. Cheryl was devastated. A friend told her he had left for Washington DC, to begin a job with one of the big environmental organizations. He had made his plans without saying a word to her.

Todd's callous abandonment hit her hard and she went into a tailspin. A few weeks later, Cheryl found herself back in her childhood bedroom, surrounded by cardboard boxes from her college apartment. She hardly left the room for a month. Her parents were bewildered. Cheryl was too humiliated to tell them how she had been dumped. Despite her hurt and anger at his betrayal, she came to realize that she still wanted to fight climate change any way she could. It was the obvious thing that she, and everyone, should be doing. Also, she had a fantasy of someday proving to Todd what he was missing.

Now, ten years later, she had gone into another tailspin, when she was fired from her latest job. After a few months, the only work she had found was delivering pizzas. She cut back on every expense she could think of. She ended her donations to C4 and even stopped buying from the organic food co-op, the last vestige of her commitment to socially responsible consumption. She was reduced to buying processed junk on sale from a big supermarket. Without a steady job, the bills kept piling up and the threat of eviction from her apartment was real. What would she do without this place where she could hide from the world whenever she needed to? Amy's rock-solid support and encouragement helped Cheryl keep her hope alive—but just barely.

When her cousin Bob, the only person in the family who was consistently nice to her, called to tell her about an opening at Success Dynamics, the company he worked for, she listened. And because she trusted Bob, she agreed to the interview. Cheryl didn't understand exactly what Success Dynamics did, only that it was a big company that provided services to even bigger companies, the ones that were destroying the future. Years after her college promise to herself to never sell out, she had finally reached the bottom.

Tomorrow morning, her sellout would be complete.

ORIENTATION

THE STRANGER IN THE MIRROR stared back at Cheryl. She was wearing a stylishly-cut gray blazer over a cream-colored blouse and black pants, the combination that Amy had picked out for the first day of the new job. Cheryl shook her head slowly in dismay. This outfit made her sellout all too real. She tied the bright blue scarf around her neck and tucked it into the blouse—the touch that Amy assured her would complete the look and make it "pop." Above the stranger's outfit, she was the same old Cheryl. Amy had urged her to wear some makeup, "it wouldn't kill you to add a little color," and even brought a basic makeup kit to Cheryl's apartment. Cheryl adamantly refused. She hadn't worn makeup for ten years and wasn't about to start now. "Who knows what kind of poison is in that stuff!" The worst part was that makeup was a racket, a conspiracy to exploit female self-hatred. "They want you to cover up your real face so you can be more 'attractive' to men. All that does is force women to compete with each other. It's sick and I don't want any part of it." The last time she wore makeup or lipstick was in college, when it hadn't done her much good. Todd walked out on her anyway.

She looked into the mirror one more time after she put on her new overcoat. *Here goes nothing.*

As she drove west on Interstate 44 for the eighteen mile trip from her apartment in south St. Louis, she noted with relief that the rush hour traffic was headed the other direction. Still, she was haunted by the thought of how much this long daily commute would increase her personal carbon footprint. She had had many jobs over the past ten years, but never one this far away.

After college, Cheryl's parents were on her case to get a job and live frugally so she could pay down her student loans. They also thought that work would be the best way for her to get over the mysterious funk that baffled them. She wouldn't talk about Todd and what had happened— getting dumped was way too shameful.

She had lost all interest in chemistry and refused to apply for jobs in the industry. She went to work for a series of nonprofits, the only employers that met her new standards of social responsibility—including a day care center, an artisanal bakery collective, and an animal shelter. The pay was always lousy, but she could feel virtuous. She devoted her free time to volunteering with C4. She went to meetings and demonstrations and kept reading about the intensifying climate crisis night after night.

Each of Cheryl's jobs started with high hopes, then ended in disappointment. She was good at every task that was put in front of her, but working with people was another story. She got anxious easily, then found fault with her bosses and coworkers, and began making critical comments or launching into tirades about climate change. She didn't know how to pick up the cues when she was causing trouble for herself. The methods Dr. Pettus had taught her in high school usually evaporated when she got triggered.

After seven years of jobs with a long string of nonprofits, she was still living in her parents' house, had almost no savings, and was making student loan payments that barely covered the ever-accumulating interest. So she relaxed her standard for acceptable employers to include small, local businesses. It was the beginning of her sellout, but she had to do something different. She landed work as the office manager for a family-owned plumbing contractor and was, as usual, good at it—answering phone calls, scheduling plumbers, sending out invoices, and ordering supplies, She kept everything organized and always had answers to the owner's questions. Most of the job could be done alone or by phone, which helped her hold her anxiety in check. And she learned to keep her mouth shut.

The plumbing company paid more than she had ever earned and the money allowed her to begin whittling down her student loan balance and get a small apartment near the corner of Louisiana and Cherokee in an older part of St. Louis city—a neighborhood her family members thought was dangerous. She bought a used Prius, cheap because of a few dents, and was even able to make regular donations to C4. They weren't much, but she felt good she was doing her part.

Cheryl's apartment became the place where she could be alone as much as she wanted, which was a lot of the time. Within a year, she felt confident enough to have a semi-satisfactory relationship with a boyfriend, Derek, which lasted through a winter. She met him at a bar on South Grand she had gone to with Amy. A month later, they were spending evenings in her apartment making dinner, watching TV, and cuddling. She soaked up his warmth and softness. Every hour with him pushed memories of Todd further into the rearview mirror. He was pretty quiet, which she liked at first. But after a few months, they ran out of things to talk about. Derek wasn't interested in climate change, protests, or much else and Cheryl realized that she was a lot smarter than him. He lived with his parents, so he wanted to spend night after night at her place—and started hanging his clothes in her closet and leaving his toothbrush, shampoo, and comb in her bathroom. That got on her nerves and she began to feel claustrophobic. So, one evening she told him to leave. He looked sad and surprised, but he didn't argue. After he walked out the door with all his stuff, the apartment felt like it was hers again. For the next two years, she had her haven.

Then, four months ago, everything at the plumbing company blew up in her face. She got into an argument with the owner's son, an entitled brat and party boy—also a lousy plumber—who was waiting to take over the business when his father retired. Cheryl confronted him about lavish expenses on the company's credit card at bars and nightclubs. A shouting match followed, and Cheryl was fired by the end of the day. She was shocked that the owner sided with his worthless son, despite the years of good work she had done.

Cheryl turned off the interstate at an exit near the edge of the St. Louis metropolitan area, where subdivisions and shopping malls began to give way to farms and forests. She had driven past this place countless times over the years, but never gave it a second thought until her recent interview. She saw the sprawling corporate campus along the frontage road. One building had a large logo on a wall for passing vehicles to see: an S intertwined with a D, with the rest of "Success Dynamics Inc." trailing out behind.

She pulled her dented Prius into the huge parking lot and found a visitor's spot. With its faded paint and an unruly collection of bumper stickers plastered on its rear, for every environmental cause and liberal candidate imaginable, her car stood out like a sore thumb amidst the long rows of late model SUVs and pickups—gas guzzlers all. Cheryl walked toward a building for her orientation appointment with Human Resources. She felt self-conscious in her brand-new "bulletproof" outfit.

She pushed through a revolving glass door into a carpeted lobby, where a video screen filled the wall behind the receptionist's desk. A collage of soft-focus images continuously unfolded: happy families playing together, happy salespeople with happy customers, happy golfers out on the course, happy parents dropping happy children off at school, happy mothers preparing dinner in perfect kitchens. Cheryl introduced herself to the receptionist and sat on a sofa in front of a glass coffee table with large photo books, *Your Cherished Dreams*, *Wishes Do Come True*, and *Welcome To The Good Life*. She opened one and saw that it was a catalog of luxury items. Instead of a price in dollars, the description of each item listed the number of points required.

After a few minutes, an elevator door opened and a woman walked out. Her wide smile radiated enthusiasm. She was tall with soft, but precise, hair and a tailored, casual suit. She appeared to be younger than Cheryl and was wearing red lipstick, eyeliner, and a faint wash of color on her cheeks. Amy would have approved.

"Welcome to Success Dynamics, Ms. Ricard. Glad to have you on the team. I'm Heather Holmes. Follow me upstairs and we'll get you started on your new career!"

The elevator door opened to reveal another video wall in front of Human Resources, which flashed photos of smiling Success Dynamics employees at work at computers, on telephones, in meetings, and in a warehouse. Heather led Cheryl into a conference room, offered her coffee and pastries, and explained how the day would go: paperwork, a brief orientation video, basic training on Cheryl's company-issued phone and laptop, then lunch in a private dining room with Paul Boland and his team.

While Cheryl filled out a stack of forms and got her picture taken for her company ID badge, she listened to Heather's chirpy patter about the many perks and delights of working for Success Dynamics Inc., or SDI for short: a huge selection of delicious food in the main cafeteria, at very attractive prices; workout rooms with showers, free Pilates, Zumba, and yoga classes; fun events after work almost every week and fantastic discounts on items in the catalog. "I've furnished my entire house with them!" A nearby car repair shop offered both special prices to SDI people and a courtesy shuttle so their cars could be serviced while they were at work. "You name it, we have it!"

Heather paused and Cheryl suddenly realized that she was supposed to make small talk. So she asked, "How many employees work here?"

"None!" Heather answered gleefully. "We don't have 'employees' at SDI. But more than 2,500 team members work on this campus. And now you're one of us. The newest member of the SDI family."

Heather dimmed the lights in the room and the SDI logo shimmered on a massive video screen. "This is a video we use to introduce SDI to clients, who are the lifeblood of our company. Every time I watch it, I realize how lucky I am to be an SDI team member. It's really impressive."

Upbeat music plays. A collage of video clips slide, tumble, and flip across the screen. They show people at work in various settings: a salesperson with customers in a car dealership, a technician repairing a refrigerator in a kitchen as the family looks on, an insurance agent going over a policy with a couple in their living room, construction workers in hardhats using power tools, agents on the phone in a call center, a supervisor talking to employees in a factory, a health care worker pushing a senior citizen in a wheelchair.

Narrator: These are the people who represent your company. As far as your customers are concerned, they <u>are</u> your company. So you need them to bring their A-game, day after day.

Do they have what it takes for your business to grow and prosper?

Success Dynamics Inc. has been helping companies succeed for more than sixty years. We know what makes people tick, how to reach them, and what will bring out their highest level of performance. After you set the goals your company wants to achieve, we draw upon our decades of experience working with millions of high achievers to craft a custom plan just for you. So the people who sell your products and take care of your customers will do their best, their absolute best, for you, again and again. How do we make that happen?

We motivate, we teach, and we guide the way.

We motivate:

What do the people who represent your company really want? What inspires them? What will encourage them to work a little smarter, to talk to one more customer, to put their best foot forward?

Through research and listening, we answer those questions to identify the right mix of incentives that will encourage them to go the extra mile for you. Those may include a tailored collection of rewards they will dream about. Items that improve life for them and their family. And unforgettable travel experiences that reinforce the message 'You've made it! You're a winner—the best of the best!'

We teach:

What stands in the way of success? Too often, it's a lack of accurate knowledge or a critical skill. We work alongside your internal teams so that every one of your people has what they need to be successful. From e-learning and seminars to FAQs and tip sheets, we create cost-effective tools that help them become experts who can serve your customers better than anyone else.

We guide the way:

Every successful person asks themselves "How did I do today? What can I do better tomorrow?" We take the guesswork out of tracking performance. You get reports that will help you make better decisions and, more importantly, your people get targeted feedback so they can see just where they stand and where they need to go next.

For decades, SDI has refined the art and science of success. The principles are timeless, but we keep up with changing tastes and technologies. Now, your people can have all SDI services at their fingertips twenty-four seven with our exciting new suite of mobile apps. They will be focused and in touch whenever you need them to be. Think about the possibilities. You'll have instant access to everyone who serves your customers.

That's what Success Dynamics Inc. can do for you! Let us bring our magic to your business!

The music swells to a crescendo and the Success Dynamics Inc. logo fills the screen.

The lights came up. Cheryl wasn't sure what to make of the video. She saw that Heather, with a smile, was looking at her and expecting her to say something.

"Wow. Thank you," was all Cheryl could think of.

"Impressive, right?" Heather said. "You can see why this is such an exciting company. I know you're going to love it here."

Cheryl nodded. Heather handed her a tablet. "At SDI, we value everyone's point of view, and especially the opinions of our team members. You've only been here an hour and you already have your first opportunity to make this company better. We'd like to know your reactions to the video you just saw. Take a few moments to respond to the statements on this tablet. Whatever comes to mind. There are no right or wrong answers. Click Submit when you're finished, then we'll move on to the next phase of your orientation."

Cheryl saw the first statement on the tablet, *I enjoyed this video,* with a scale from one, *Strongly Disagree,* to ten, *Strongly Agree.* This whole thing bewildered Cheryl. She didn't know what they wanted from her, so she played it safe and tapped a nine.

Next, *The video gave me a positive impression of Success Dynamics Inc.* Again, she went for the safe answer, nine.

SDI is a company with an exciting mission. Nine.

I look forward to learning more about SDI from my manager. Eight. (She didn't want every answer to be the same.)

I'm glad I made the decision to join SDI. Ten. (Why not? She was broke.)

I have a bright future with SDI. Seven. (She didn't want them to think she was a pushover.)

I look forward to telling my family and friends about the benefits of working at SDI. Eight. (The fewer people who knew she took this sellout job, the better—but no point in telling HR that.)

Human Resources is doing a great job with my orientation. With Heather sitting next to her, Cheryl figured the right response was ten.

An IT technician, Sam, entered the room with Cheryl's company-issued phone and laptop. Heather stepped out while he showed Cheryl how to use them and set up her logins. "All SDI team members have our app suite pre-installed on both devices. We're the beta testers for the latest version."

He opened the apps on both the phone and the laptop.

"*SDI Achieve* shows your progress on key performance indicators and your real-time points earnings. You can select the catalog tab to see all awards you're eligible for, along with their costs in points. Click to put awards that interest you onto your *My Dreams* list. The app will notify you when you earn enough points to redeem the awards you've selected. Don't worry, you can add or remove awards from *My Dreams* anytime."

He then went on to the *SDI KnowHow* app. "Your manager has created a custom learning plan just for you, with all the tools and resources you'll need. Because it syncs with your calendar in the *SDI YAH!* App, it can suggest learning tools that are relevant to whatever you're doing that day. You can choose to engage with the tools either on your laptop or your phone. Personally, I prefer learning from my phone while I'm working out. Super convenient!"

Finally, he showed her the third app. "*SDI YAH!*, which is short for *You Are Here*, is totally awesome." He pumped his fist when he said "YAH!"

"In addition to being your calendar, it tracks what you accomplish each day. Both you and your manager can add tasks and meetings to your calendar. It's also the vehicle for push notifications from your manager, your department head, and even Mr. M."

Cheryl was bewildered. "Who's Mr. M?"

"Randall Manifest, the CEO. He created today's SDI and guides us forward. The man is brilliant! His messages really make you think. You'll always know what's important to him and to your manager. What you're supposed to focus on. Takes a lot of guesswork out of the job. Something I really appreciate.

"And here on campus, *SDI YAH!* has an extra feature. It works like a map that can guide you from point A to B. With all the buildings in the complex, this one is super helpful. You'll never be late for a meeting!"

Heather returned, smiling as always. "The app suite is impressive, right? We're building the future at SDI."

Sam set a small plastic case on the table. "This is the latest enhancement to the apps, so far only available to SDI team members." He opened the case to reveal a small tan earbud. "A complete audio interface! You can talk to the apps and they can talk to you. You'll love it. It fits snugly in your ear and is almost invisible."

As he showed Cheryl how to use the earbud, Heather said, "Company policy is for all team members to wear their earbuds while they're working. Many of us like to wear them during off hours too. You don't want to miss anything important. Go ahead and take it for a spin."

When Cheryl activated the earbud, Heather tapped her phone. A voice came through to Cheryl. "Hello, Cheryl. Randall Manifest here. I want to personally welcome you to the SDI family. From everything I've heard about you, I know you'll be making amazing contributions to the company. You're a winner and I've got my eye on you!"

Heather saw the look of surprise on Cheryl's face and gave her a thumbs up sign. Then another voice came through the earbud. "Hey, Cheryl, this is Paul. We're so pumped that you're joining us today! I'll see you as soon as you're done with Heather and you'll meet everyone else on the team at the traditional welcome lunch."

"One other policy goes without saying," Heather said. "Your laptop and phone are strictly for company business. Not for calls, messaging, or anything else that is personal. IT monitors all traffic. And please do not show the apps—or discuss them—with anyone outside the company. We must protect our proprietary information and trade secrets. I'm sure you understand. Also, the requirements are spelled out in the confidentiality section of the employment agreement you signed."

Cheryl hadn't read the pages of fine print at the back of the documents she had signed earlier while Heather was gushing about the amazing pastries from the SDI kitchen.

Sam said. "If you have a problem with your devices, just say 'Need IT support now' and we'll be talking to you before you know it."

After Sam left, Heather said once again, "Impressive, right?" She offered to walk with Cheryl to Paul's office and said that it was a good opportunity to try out the *SDI YAH!* app. "Just say, YAH, take me to Paul Boland's office."

Cheryl was puzzled. "You just said that and it didn't do anything."

"It recognizes your voice and responds only to you."

"Already?"

"It's very smart. Doesn't take long."

Cheryl said the words and the app voice directed her out of the conference room and led her and Heather through three buildings, down one elevator, and up another until they reached Paul's office. "Impressive, right?" Heather commented for the umpteenth time as she knocked on the office door and left. "Let me know if there's any way I can help you get acclimated to your SDI future. I'm always here when you need me."

Paul came out and shook Cheryl's hand. He pointed out her cubicle, which was right outside his office, so she could put down her laptop and shoulder bag. They went back into his office and sat down. Paul looked tired. His narrow shoulders were slumped and he apologized for his disheveled desk. "There's never enough time in the day to stay on top of the incoming clutter. Also, we have twin three-year old girls at home, and another baby on the way. After I get them to bed, I usually work for another few hours. With your help, I hope to get a little more sleep."

Cheryl took notes as he described the team's responsibilities. "We handle three of SDI's biggest accounts, Mega Motors, SkyBridge Communications, and Neighborly Mutual Insurance." All were household names that Cheryl knew from TV commercials.

"Their business is worth millions of dollars a year to the company, so it's important that we do everything perfectly. We work under the leadership of the account manager for these clients, Jack Weatherly."

"Will he be at our lunch today?"

"No. He spends most of his time on the road, traveling from client to client. He'll be here next week. I told him about your fantastic experience and attention to detail and he can't wait to meet you."

A man and a woman appeared at Paul's door. "We're all here. Time for lunch," Paul said. He introduced them to Cheryl as they walked to the elevator. Mavis Rodriguez was a travel coordinator who managed travel for client events, which can involve hundreds of people, as well as travel plans for team members. She laughed, "That's ninety-eight percent Jack. He's constantly on the move and doesn't like dealing with reservations. Too much hassle for him, so he calls me. When you need to go somewhere, shoot me a message." The idea of traveling for work hadn't occurred to Cheryl. She'd never done that before.

Rick Joy was a graphic designer, who put together presentations and proposals for Jack. "He wants every communication to clients to be top-notch and on-brand. He likes to impress them with our quick turnaround of polished pieces. I'm his guy for PowerPoints, PDFs, and glossy handouts."

Paul said to Cheryl, "Of course we have to interface with many other departments at SDI to get our projects done. As you learn your way around the company, you'll be taking over a lot of that."

They got off the elevator and walked through the large employee cafeteria, where a few hundred people were carrying trays and sitting at tables. Video screens lined the wall, showing images from SDI programs and events, along with a scroll of client logos. They entered a small private dining room. A waiter stood at the door to welcome them. The linen-covered table was set for four. The waiter handed them menus and took drink orders. It was a far cry from the ramen, canned tuna, and baked beans that Cheryl would be subsisting on at home while she waited for her first paycheck to come through.

Small talk with strangers always brought Cheryl's fears and anxieties to just below the surface. She had to concentrate to smile and chat as they asked her about hobbies—"I enjoy hiking and canoeing. Anything that gets me outdoors"—and about where she lived. She described her neighborhood in the older part of the city. "I like the architecture and the walkability." She could tell that it was a surprise to the others, who all lived in newer suburbs.

Paul told Mavis and Rick about Cheryl's experience with the plumbing company. He joked, "If she can get plumbers out to fix a flooded basement in the middle of the night, nothing we have to deal with is going to faze her." Paul asked Mavis how her morning was going. "Oh, another day in paradise—with a touch of stormy weather…ly. We had tomorrow set with SkyBridge clients in Orlando—country club, VIP golf, the works. Then Jack called last night. Same clients, but a last-minute switch to pheasant shooting in North Dakota. And monogrammed hunting jackets for five people. I had to scramble, but we got it done." Mavis was the only one who ordered wine with lunch.

Rick offered to show Cheryl the projects he was working on—presentations, proposals, and flyers. "They'll give you a good idea of the look and feel we're always after."

"What do I do when I get a question from a client?" Cheryl asked.

"You won't," Paul said. "Your job is strictly behind the scenes. The only people who communicate with the clients are Jack first, then me on certain issues. SDI is a big company, but we want the clients to experience it as a small boutique, with personal attention for them and them alone. Customer intimacy and ease of doing business. That's how Jack has built a multimillion-dollar portfolio of clients. Our job is to deliver on his promises."

"He makes a lot of promises," Mavis interjected, as she sipped her Chardonnay.

Paul continued without missing a beat. "We have five or six balls in the air all the time. I'm counting on you never to drop one. Jack hates cleaning up our messes."

After lunch, Paul had a long list of phone calls to make, so Cheryl started to plow through the stack of papers and folders on her desk. Her email inbox already had fifty messages. Rick, whose cubicle was next to hers, gave her a tip. "People here like to copy everyone under the sun on their emails. After a little while, you'll figure out which ones you can safely ignore."

An automated message chirped in her earbud. "You're off to a great start, Cheryl. Need help organizing your files?"

"No, thanks."

"Some useful tips are in your notifications box when you want them." Cheryl spent hours reading, sorting, and filing. She began to get a picture of what was going on with each of the team's three clients, but ended with more questions than answers.

Late in the day, Paul waved for her to come into his office and close the door. "I got a call from HR. It's about your car. There have been complaints about the way it looks. Some people wondered what it was doing in the SDI parking lot." He swiveled his laptop so she could see a photo of the bumper stickers. "Whatever you do on your own time is your business. But we like to keep politics off campus. Teamwork is the key to our success." Cheryl was dumbfounded. "What am I supposed to do? It's the only car I have."

"Can you take the bumper stickers off?"

"That'll ruin the paint job!"

"You're going to be a valuable member of the team. But please, don't put anything else on your car." Cheryl was pissed. *If they had built this place in the city with access to public transportation, no one would have to worry about what my car looks like!*

Paul took out a map of the SDI campus and pointed to a distant corner of the parking lot behind the warehouse loading docks. "From now on, park your car here, where nobody will see it. OK?" Cheryl reminded herself how much she needed this job. So she nodded *yes* and kept her mouth shut.

Paul's phone rang. He mouthed "Jack" to her and gestured that she should leave. As she walked back to her cubicle, she heard him saying "Yes. Uh-huh I'll get that information to you right away. I'm on it, Jack."

At home that evening, Cheryl was exhausted, drained by the long day of interacting with people. And the apps chattering to her through the earbud creeped her out. Her phone rang—it was Amy. "I'll swing by and pick you up for tonight's meeting. Afterwards, we can grab some drinks at that club on Kingshighway with the cute bartender. You can tell me about the first day at the new job."

Cheryl had completely forgotten about the monthly C4 chapter planning session. She begged off. "It's been crazy. I can't handle any more." Also, she was embarrassed about the SDI job and dreaded the thought of people at C4 finding out about it. (*I look forward to telling my family and friends about the benefits of working at SDI. Not on your life!*)

"Have it your way. But the planet isn't going to save itself."

Cheryl heated up leftovers for dinner and sat on her sofa skipping through Netflix and TV channels, searching for a comforting, mindless diversion. As she clicked the remote, she realized she could handle the SDI job. And she was curious about this guy Jack, the so far invisible man who was yanking everyone's chain.

The Grand Tour

Cheryl arrived at SDI early Tuesday morning. She found the parking space Paul had told her to use—behind a row of industrial-sized dumpsters next to the loading docks, twice as far from her office as other empty spaces in the main lot. It was annoying to trudge past the late-model gas guzzlers on her long walk to the main entrance. But she knew she had to suck it up for the sake of her apartment.

As soon as she entered the building, a message popped up on her phone that her campus tour would begin this afternoon—and reminded her to wear her earbud all day. Paul wasn't in the office yet, so she straightened the mess on his desk, careful not to make it hard for him to find anything. Bringing order to his office was just as satisfying as she had imagined during her interview. When he came in later, he looked at his desk with confusion, then went to her cubicle and asked "Did you do that?"

"Yes. I hope it makes your day easier." He was puzzled, but appreciative. "Uhm, thanks."

Paul had a series of meetings that would last all day, so Cheryl spent the morning working alone, which was soothing. She finished reviewing the files on the three accounts Jack ran and sorted them into organized categories. No one bothered her and her phone didn't ring. Mercifully, even her earbud remained quiet, except for telling her about a short training on *How to Make the*

Most of Your Onboarding Experience. She listened for a bit while going through her files, but the tips were obvious and not much help. *Introduce yourself to everyone you meet. Ask questions. Be ready to discuss your experience with your manager.* Cheryl put her phone on mute part way through to silence the useless advice, so she could work in peace. At noon, she ate a peanut butter and jelly sandwich at her desk and made notes about the projects she was reviewing. The *SDI YAH!* app alerted her it was time to leave for the first of the four stops on her afternoon campus tour of Research, Rewards, Stagecraft, and Post-Production.

The app guided her to the lowest level of the building, then through a tunnel to a different building, where she entered an elevator and pressed the button for the Research floor. When the door opened to reveal the lobby, she saw a video screen full of smiling people wearing headsets in a call center, a focus group around a conference table, and colorful animated graphs and charts. Words floated across the screen proclaiming *What Do Your Customers Value? What Motivates Your Sales Force? What Moves the Needle? We Develop Insights You Can Use.*

The receptionist looked up and smiled. "Welcome to Research, Ms. Ricard. Mr. Ricard will be here shortly."

Cousin Bob walked in with a broad smile. "I'm so glad to see you, Cheryl. You're going to love it here at SDI."

Cheryl was happy to see a familiar face, someone she'd known her whole life, in this strange place. Bob was twelve years older than Cheryl. His father and her father were first cousins. As a kid, Cheryl looked up to him as someone who was smoother and more sophisticated than her working class parents and older siblings. His branch of the family had all been to college and pursued "careers."

As they walked past nondescript offices, he explained Research's function within SDI. "Our mission is to understand what people want. A fascinating field. We study customer satisfaction. What they like and don't like, and what motivates them to buy. Think about it. Do you like your phone company? What do you think they do well? What do you hate about them? How could they make you like them more? Our most important business, something SDI does better than anyone else, is employee research— what will motivate people to work harder and smarter? How much do they actually care about their company? You'd be surprised at how little even the biggest companies know about their employees, especially the people in their channel."

"Their what?"

"The channel is all the people and companies between you and your customers. For example, when you buy a can of tomato soup, you don't buy it from Campbell's. You buy it from a supermarket, which also didn't buy it from Campbell's. They bought it from a distributor. At each step along the way, people are making decisions about what to buy and what to sell. Does the distributor recommend Campbell's to the supermarket buyer? Or a competitor's soup? What price promotions will the distributor offer? What deals will end up in the supermarket's weekly flyer? These decisions get complicated really fast. How can the CEO of Campbell's influence all the people between him, in his office on the fortieth floor somewhere, and you, the customer in the supermarket? We try to understand all the pieces of the puzzle so we can help our clients figure out what they can do to nudge the people who have leverage to push their product and not the competitor's."

"Can't they just offer them more money?"

"They could, but that may not be the best way to do it. What SDI discovered years ago is that the right rewards will get people to work harder at a lower cost than just paying them more money. The trick is identifying what those rewards are—and they're different for each person. What appeals to a thirty-year-old air conditioning installer isn't the same as what appeals to the forty-five-year-old salesperson who sold the system. We do surveys, interviews, and focus groups—all the traditional methods. But they have a significant flaw. When you ask people what motivates them, their responses can be based on wishful thinking or their desire to express socially acceptable preferences, how they want to be seen by others. We're developing a proprietary method that yields fantastic data on what actually motivates individuals, as opposed to what they say motivates them. Our clients are very excited about it. It could be a game changer."

He opened a door marked *CVD 1.* A desk with a computer display was in the center of the room. Another desk, covered with equipment, was in the corner. "This is a comparative value discriminator, or CVD. The subject responds to a series of side-by-side images of different items that appear on the screen. It moves quickly, so they have to go with first impressions and not spend time analyzing. Simultaneously, we measure the strength of their autonomic nervous system reactions—how their body is responding. The combined accuracy is amazing."

"Is this what you've been working on? All you ever said at the family parties was 'market research.'"

"Now that you've signed the SDI confidentiality agreement, I can talk about it. Let's see what the CVD can tell us about the motivations of Cheryl Ricard."

He led her to the desk in the center of the room, then picked up some cables from the other desk. "I'm going to attach these sensors to your head and arms."

Cheryl looked at him with alarm, "No way!"

Bob laughed. "Relax. They won't hurt. This is easier than getting your blood pressure taken." Cheryl took a deep breath to push her anxiety down. She disliked being touched, but Bob was family. She kept breathing slowly as he affixed the sensors with tape, then sat at the other desk and tapped the keyboard. "First, we calibrate the system."

An aroma of lilacs wafted through the room. Cheryl smiled. A few seconds later, the sulfuric stench of rotten eggs replaced it. She grimaced. "Smell is the sense that is least affected by cognitive processes and cultural influences," Bob said. "This gives us a baseline of how your body reacts to pleasant and unpleasant stimuli. It calibrates the system for a more accurate measurement of your responses to the visual stimuli."

He explained that the monitor will display pairs of images of various items next to each other. "Each will only be up for a few seconds. Touch the item you prefer. You'll get the hang of it in no time." He dimmed the lights and the images began. The first pair was a birthday cake and a broken window. That was easy. Next came a coffee table and a floor lamp. Cheryl chose the floor lamp—she already had a coffee table. Then, a blender and a barbecue grill, followed by a bicycle and a set of golf clubs. The images flashed in rapid-fire succession. Some of the pairs didn't make sense, like a woman on a diving board next to a roast turkey on a platter. How was she supposed to pick between those? If she couldn't decide and hesitated, a loud beep sounded, and another pair of images appeared. She had to concentrate to keep up. After about fifty pairs, the final images were a children's birthday party and a mountain meadow. She chose the meadow, then saw words on the screen, *Thank you for your responses.* Cheryl let out a sigh of relief as the lights came back up.

As Bob removed the sensors, he said, "We use this tool to gather data on the psychographics of program participant groups. We'll have your analysis in a few seconds." The computer printed out a report and Bob and Cheryl looked at it together. It summarized: *Subject presents a strong preference for the natural environment and outdoor activities. Subject also has an aversion to social gatherings and is most comfortable when alone. Home furnishings and electronic entertainment systems have little appeal to Subject. Products marketed as "green" or "environmentally friendly" have strong appeal for Subject.* The rest of the report was a long, detailed table of preference values.

"Sounds like my Cheryl," he joked. "Don't worry, I'll delete all your data."

After saying goodbye to Bob, Cheryl followed the earbud's directions out of Research to her next destination, Rewards. She crossed the parking lot on the way to the huge, windowless SDI warehouse. It felt good to be outside under a clear, blue sky. She realized that, on the SDI campus, she was likely to spend entire days without setting foot outdoors. She saw a line of trucks parked at a long loading dock and the app directed her to the far side of the building, not too far from the place Paul made her park, where a sign that said *Rewards* was mounted above a door. She entered a lobby with another huge video screen. Images of workers picking boxes off warehouse shelves were interspersed with delighted families unpacking the prizes delivered to their homes. The earbud told her "You've arrived! Your appointment is with Doug Ellison." The receptionist, who received the same announcement in her earbud, welcomed Cheryl and directed her to a chair. A few minutes later, a man with thin, slicked-back hair and a crisp blue shirt strode briskly into the room. He smiled with gleaming white teeth as he shook Cheryl's hand enthusiastically—a little too enthusiastically for her comfort. "Welcome to Rewards, Ms. Ricard! I'm Doug Ellison, Director of Reward Strategies. Let's get started!" As they walked up a flight of stairs, then down a long corridor, he said "Rewards is the beating heart of SDI. Every program we do and every great result we achieve for our clients is rooted in our unique philosophy of incentives."

They entered a conference room with a large, polished table and a curtain covering one wall. "Ms. Ricard, or may I call you Cheryl?" He didn't wait for a reply before continuing, "Why are you here?" Cheryl was a little confused by the question. "This is part of my orientation tour."

"No. Why are you here at SDI? Why did you take this job?"

"I need to make a living."

"So you're here for a paycheck?"

"I guess so."

"And is that paycheck going to cause you to give your absolute best every day you're at work?"

"Uhhmmm…"

"Be honest now. Don't worry, I won't tell HR what you say." He waited with a grin and twinkling eyes. Cheryl felt trapped. She had no idea what was going on. After a moment of trepidation, she stammered "I'm responsible and take my work seriously. I do whatever I'm asked to do. And the paycheck is part of the bargain."

"But will you do *more* than you're asked? Will you give SDI every ounce of your initiative and creativity? Will you come in early and stay late? Will you look for new ways to do your job better? I submit that you won't. Money alone won't bring out your best effort. Money alone won't lead you to become the best person you can be! I don't say this as a criticism of you, Cheryl. It's human nature, true for everyone, even for me."

Now, Cheryl was totally confused. She thought big corporations were all about money. *Where is this guy going?*

"Think back to the dawn of human history. Back before this weird thing called money was invented. What motivated our ancestors? What got them out of the cave to hunt? What got them to fight fiercely for their families? A delicious roast leg of antelope. A bearskin to keep them and their children warm at night. A pouch decorated with shells and beads for the tribal dance. All things they could see and touch, not the sterile abstraction of a bank account. Humans evolved to want things we can hold and feel, experiences we can savor. When presented properly, those can move us so much more than money alone. Money is necessary, but not sufficient. It just gets you closer to the things that really matter. Human beings need to see and be seen. SDI's brilliant discovery is that this same principle applies to modern business. Tangible rewards are what bring out the best in people. We call it trophy value. Remember that term. It's what motivates each client's employees, distributors, dealers, and retailers to do *more* than they're asked when they sell the client's products and take care of the client's customers. These rewards are the most powerful business tool ever devised for increasing sales and profits! And you, Cheryl, are now part of this amazing work, which truly makes lives better. All of us are happiest and most fulfilled when we have something real and solid to strive for, something that we can show off with pride and say 'I'm a winner because I earned this!'"

Doug's eyes glowed with triumphant fire as he finished his speech. He waited for Cheryl's response, but she was too stunned to say anything. *What have I gotten myself into?* He stood up and motioned for her to follow him to the curtain-covered wall. He pushed a button and the curtain parted to reveal a long window that overlooked the massive warehouse, a humming beehive of activity. Workers moved up and down on telescoping scaffolds to pick boxes off multilevel shelving and place them in automated carts that scurried through the aisles.

"Behold! We're injecting adrenaline into the bloodstream of American business. Spreading the magic of dreams fulfilled to the hundreds of thousands of people who benefit from our programs. Every day, trucks fan out from this warehouse carrying a curated collection of rewards that spell success in many languages—that of the mechanic, the insurance agent, the delivery driver, the repair technician, the computer programmer, and, most of all, the salesperson. Each reward nudges a participant in an SDI program to work a little harder, to stretch themselves a little farther, to overcome their internal limits and put out what we call 'discretionary effort,' that which we don't have to do to keep our job, but which we *can* do to excel, to make our lives better. When thousands of people each choose to do a little bit more, day after day, their efforts add up to increased profit for our clients."

Doug pointed to the award catalogs spread out on the table. Some were new, others were from decades past. "SDI pioneered the award catalog concept many years ago and we have continually refined our catalogs to enhance their irresistible appeal. When a participant opens the catalog created just for them and their company, they see their best life on every page, waiting for them to do just a bit more today at work. To come up with a better idea and put it into action, to call one more customer, to ask one more question, to *care*. Because the catalog tells them that success, just the way they imagine it, is within their grasp. Today they can get one step closer and tomorrow can bring them closer still.

"We like the printed catalog, because it entices the participant's family to look through it again and again and keeps the goal top of mind." He picks up a phone from the table. "Now we have evolved to the technology that people expect today—a personalized catalog in their pocket, even in the pockets of the spouse and children. Where it will remind and inspire as they go through their day. When they complete a task, when a customer gives them a rating, they can see instantly how their personal score goes up." He kept talking as he pulled up a photo of a gas grill on the phone. The app spoke, *Congratulations, you're fifty-two percent of the way to winning the gourmet grill. You have earned 8,354 points toward the 16,000 points you need. Today, you got 162 points closer. Make tomorrow an even better day!*

"The catalog app becomes embedded in their daily routine as the trusted, encouraging friend who is helping them reach their potential, to become the person they want to be"

He clicked on another photo from the catalog, a television. "Here's what a teenager might see and hear. *Mom did a great job today. She's working hard so we can watch our favorite movies on this sixty-five inch TV with surround sound and the subwoofer. Give her a hug!'*

Doug beamed with pride as he set the phone down. Cheryl wasn't sure what he wanted, but figured she better say something. "How do you customize the catalog?"

"Great question! Have you been to the Research department yet?"

"Right before I came here."

"They do brilliant stuff—all way over my head. We use their data to create a custom awards catalog for each client. In the future, we will be able to tailor the catalog to each individual. Think of that! Every page will say to them, 'This is what you want, and you can have it if you work a little smarter, a little harder. Because you, and only you, control your destiny.' Have you looked at your personal catalog yet?"

"No. This is only my second day on the job."

"You're going to love it! And if it doesn't have everything you ever desired, let me know."

Doug stood up to shake Cheryl's hand. The meeting was over. "Who exactly do you work for?"

"Paul Boland. Our team supports Jack Weatherly."

Doug's eyebrows raised in surprise. "Weatherly? The man's a genius! More selling talent in his little finger than the rest of the company combined. You'll learn a lot from him. I'm envious."

Cheryl left the Rewards building in a daze, her head spinning from Doug's wild diatribe. She tapped her phone and heard the directions to the next stop on her tour, Stagecraft. The breeze on her face helped her calm down as she crossed the parking lot towards another windowless building. She entered a door marked *Stagecraft* and found herself in an empty lobby. The video screens showed dancers cavorting around a new refrigerator as lights swept a stage, engineers and editors in high-tech control rooms, and speakers at podiums. Cheryl's earbud said, "You've arrived. Your contact will join you shortly."

After a few minutes, an interior door opened and a middle-aged woman approached. "Cheryl Ricard? I'm

Mary Ann Cerullo. I'm here to show you around." They shook hands. "Sorry, but we only have a receptionist on days when clients are expected. On other days, we're not important enough." Mary Ann carried a clipboard, and reading glasses dangled from a thin chain around her neck. As they walked down a corridor, she explained that she was a producer who handled everything from live shows to video shoots and voiceover recordings. They entered a cavernous, empty sound stage, with lights hanging from the ceiling, more lights on stands, and a video camera on a large dolly. "Do you make movies and TV shows here?" Cheryl asked.

Mary Ann laughed. "No, but we could. Everything we do is custom work for SDI clients. Last year, we shot a series of training videos for Pizza Barn. We built an entire restaurant in here, including the kitchen. Everything worked, except the ovens." Mary Ann pointed to the back wall, which was painted bright green. "Do you know what green screen is?" Cheryl shook her head no. "We can shoot actors in front of that wall, then edit in any background we want. Make it look like they're in the Grand Canyon, at the beach, or on the moon."

"Wow!"

Mary Ann pointed to a couple of director's chairs in a corner. "Do you mind if we sit down? I have a gimpy knee. So we're not interrupted, can you turn off your phone and remove your earbud?"

"HR told me I'm supposed to wear it all the time."

"You'll be fine. HR acts like they're all-powerful, but they don't have the capacity to track earbud use. Nothing will happen." Cheryl powered off the phone and put the earbud in a pocket.

"It's always a good idea to turn off your phones when you want to have an honest conversation with someone. So,

Cheryl, tell me about yourself." Cheryl explained that she had been hired for the team that supported Jack Weatherly. Mary Ann rolled her eyes and shook her head. "You're in for a very…interesting time with him."

"Why? Is he going to hit on me?"

Mary Ann chuckled. "Jack wouldn't do anything like that, but he has plenty of other ways of making your life miserable. Let's just say that he's…mercurial. Have you ever been to a rodeo and watched a bull rider?"

"No."

"Check YouTube and you'll see. That's what working for Weatherly is like. He's the bull and you're the rider. Expect the unexpected."

Mary Ann got two bottles of water out of a cooler and handed one to Cheryl. "Where else have you been on your campus tour?"

"Research first, then Rewards. Doug Ellison showed me the warehouse and the catalogs."

"Dougie? They let Dougie talk to you?"

Cheryl nodded her head yes.

"Oh my God, does HR want you to run screaming out of the building in your first week on the job? Don't get me wrong. Dougie's a smart guy, but he's a fanatic. He not only drinks the Kool-Aid, he serves it up in a crystal goblet. As far as Dougie's concerned, if you have the right mix of rewards with trophy value, you can cure cancer."

"He said Jack Weatherly was a genius."

"Dougie is also a world class ass kisser."

Cheryl laughed. It was a relief to meet a normal person! She let her guard down and they small talked for a while. Mary Ann had been around the block a few times at SDI and nothing bothered her. She warned Cheryl who to watch out for and gave her tips on how to avoid getting other people's work dumped on her plate. "Everyone's looking to pass the buck to someone else. Tell them what they want to hear, but keep it vague, then take care of whatever is required to head off the shitstorm. Do that a few times and then you become indispensable. They'll appreciate the lack of a shitstorm, but will probably take credit themselves."

Mary Ann offered to take her to the next stop on her tour, *Post-Production*. They walked past a row of sound booths where voice actors were recording narration tracks for training videos. She pointed out one of them. "She's the annoying voice of *SDI YAH!* in your earbud." They went up a flight of stairs. "I want you to meet one of the wizards who lives in here. He's just about my favorite person in this company." They saw video editing suites behind glass walls, where editors worked at consoles surrounded by high-tech equipment, and arrived at a door labeled *Final Sound*. Mary Ann opened the door for Cheryl and they entered a control room. A man with long, red hair in a ponytail sat with his back to the door, working at a huge console covered with computers and screens that flashed bouncing graphs and waveforms.

Mary Ann tapped Cheryl on the shoulder and motioned for her to be quiet. They watched the man's fingers dance from keyboard to mouse to trackball as he trimmed, tweaked, and repositioned snippets of sound. He tapped a screen and a voice boomed *"the future."* He tapped again and the voice blurped in reverse. He gently pulled it forward and backward with his finger on a trackball. *"is …now!"* to find the perfect spot. He tapped to mark it. He rolled his chair over to another computer which controlled effects. He tried different intensities of reverb and lengths of sustain, *"now-w-w-w. now-w-w-w-w-w,"* until he found the one he liked. He rolled his chair back to the console and tapped a keyboard to play the complete phrase *"At Mega Motors, the future is now-w-w-w-w."* Then he played the voice mixed with dramatic music. The pace wasn't quite right. He played the voice track again and paused it after *"At Mega Motors."* He rolled the trackball with the tip of his finger to lengthen the pause. *"At Mega Motors…The future."* After adjusting the pause slightly, he played it again. With his head crooked to the side, he listened intently while he rolled the trackball back and forth to find the perfect length for the pause. Satisfied, he tapped a keyboard to play the music mixed with the voice track. The longer pause after "Motors" allowed a flourish of the music to come through before the voice said *"the future is now."* Cheryl didn't understand what he was doing, but she could tell that the slight change made it better. *Wow!*

He tapped the keyboard again, then rolled his chair back to watch the video monitor suspended above his console. Gorgeous shots with dramatic lighting showed sleek sports cars and muscular pickup trucks zooming down highways, swerving on narrow mountain roads, and driving on a beach, as the music swelled and the voice boomed. *"At Mega Motors…the future is now!…"* When *"now"* echoed and faded into the music, the two interlocking M's of the Mega Motors logo appeared on the screen, shimmering metal shapes that slowly rotated as the music reached its final crescendo.

"Jeremy?" said Mary Ann. The man swiveled in his chair. He was startled. He smiled when he saw her. "You've done it again." she said. "Your usual magic. I'd like you to meet Cheryl Ricard, who's just joined the company." He stood up to shake Cheryl's hand "Jeremy Lichtman." He was wearing a black T-shirt with *Inscrutable* written in white letters across the front.

"It's not easy to make these blowhards sound good, but somebody's got to do it. After I'm done, they assume it always sounded that way. That's the problem with this work. When you do it right, no one can tell you did anything."

Mary Ann and Jeremy led Cheryl out of the mixing suite to the preview room. Mary Ann explained that this was where SDI executives, account managers, and project teams joined with clients to review final audiovisual productions for approval. Ninety-six inch flat panel monitors lined one wall. Egg carton-like acoustic tiles covered the ceiling and stacks of exotic audio speakers were arranged in a corral around two leather sofas. Some hung from the ceiling, while others were large, thin ribbons of plastic on black metal pedestals. "When clients are here, we have interns, kids doing grunt work in hopes of gaining a foothold in the business, serve platters of snacks and take drink orders." Jeremy pointed Cheryl down to one of the leather sofas. "Time for the 'wow' demo. You'll experience the full splendor of what we can conjure up."

Cheryl settled into the sofa as the lights dimmed. She saw the night sky full of stars on the huge video displays. Soft chirps and the buzz of insects surrounded her, and she was transported to a mountain meadow at dawn. The sun peeked over craggy peaks and rays of golden light bathed her. The insect sounds gave way to a magisterial string quartet. The deep moan of a cello thrummed into Cheryl's chest. Sympathetic vibrations thrilled her from the top of her head to the tips of her toes. She had never heard anything like it.

The wow demo continued with images of suburban streets, office towers, men unloading trucks and driving forklifts, all to show the vital energy of business, the relentless, urgent drive to succeed. Then leisure—mothers playing frisbee with their children in a park, fathers tossing delighted toddlers into the air. The demo concluded with evening. Well-dressed patrons in a concert hall listened to a jazz combo improvise. Then parents put their children to bed, enjoyed glasses of wine, and looked at gorgeous pictures of their next dream vacation in a catalog. At the end, a title appeared on the screen, *A day in the life, with better days to come.*

The lights came up. Cheryl was smiling. It was the most beautiful video she had ever experienced. Jeremy saw her reaction, flashed a devilish smile, and joked that his "ultra, ultra surround sound" would be illegal if the government knew how it affected listeners.

"When clients see this," Jeremy said, "they believe that we can do anything. We turn their sordid, money-grubbing businesses into matchless splendor and move their employees to push themselves to work harder and harder, drawn like moths to these shining fantasies."

"We also manage to have some fun here on the Island of Misfit Toys," said Mary Ann. She pointed upstairs to indicate SDI management. "They need us, so they mostly leave us alone. We're the only ones who know how to create the magic. Yes, we do it in service of the company and the clients. But they would be nothing without us, even though they would never admit it."

Jeremy added "We're like a guild of medieval weavers making spectacular tapestries for the walls of the king's dining hall. Our tapestries will long outlive the king. But it's not a good idea to question the king. We give him what he wants and make it much better than he expects."

"Why do you work so hard at it if the king doesn't care?" Cheryl asked.

He pointed to the control room behind the glass wall. "We get to play with the latest and best equipment there is—all day long. But mostly it's M-O-N-E-Y, scraps from the king's table. SDI pays pretty well. Isn't that why you're here?"

Cheryl had to admit that yes, it was.

"Welcome to the club!" Mary Ann said with a laugh.

Jeremy smiled. "I don't know why HR sent you to us. We're going to corrupt your innocent mind if you give us half a chance."

Mary Ann told Jeremy, "She works for Weatherly."

"That prima donna! He thinks whatever he wants is the word of God. And he changes his mind at the drop of a hat."

"Here's a classic Weatherly story," Mary Ann said. "Every time we have a final mix of a video ready for approval, he brings his clients here to review it. He acts like the lord of the manor as he shepherds them to the sofas and makes sure they have whatever snacks and drinks they desire. Then he grandly calls for us to roll the video."

"Of course, the mix is perfect," Jeremy said. "I only do perfect."

Mary Ann continued. "The clients are in awe. I watch them beaming, grinning, and looking at each other. They enthusiastically approve the mix. That's when Weatherly speaks up. He points out some imaginary flaw or other, like the bass was too loud here or a pause was too long there, and has us replay that section. He gets a serious look on his face and tells us to adjust whatever problem he found, ASAP. He reassures his client that he won't rest until every detail is absolutely correct. They're a little bewildered because it sounded fine to them. He makes sure they're listening as he gives me detailed instructions and drops in a few technical terms that he's heard from Jeremy. I take notes and say we'll take care of it by the next day. Then he escorts the clients out."

"Does that make extra work for you?" Cheryl asked. Mary Ann and Jeremy laughed.

"We don't do anything. We leave it as it was. It was already perfect. Weatherly is just putting on an act for the client to show them how much he cares about their production. He never comes back to listen to it again anyway."

At the end of the visit, Mary Ann said "When things get tough or weird—which they will—remember, you can always talk to me."

"Ditto," Jeremy said. "Whenever the company becomes too much for you, come here for a little R&R. I'm usually working late into the night."

Cheryl had expected everyone at the company to be slick corporate shills or right wing firebrands. She was surprised to find that there were some nice people who seemed glad to welcome her. *This job may not turn out to be so bad after all.*

Settling In

On Wednesday, Cheryl took a deep dive into the team's projects. During a long session in Paul's office, he answered every question she had written down on her notepad, then walked her through the open issues with Mega Motors, SkyBridge Communications, and Neighborly Mutual. She filled a different notepad for each client as she populated her to-do list with items color-coded by priority—red for *Immediate Action*, orange for *Within 3 Days*, yellow for *Within 7 Days*, and green for *As Time Permits*. The list was soon splattered in reds and oranges, with a handful of yellows, and only two greens—completing the onboarding activities required by HR and nominating team members for awards. Cheryl was relieved when Paul said "Forget the HR stuff. Let's focus on plugging holes in our leaky boat." After he left for the day to get home to his wife and toddlers, she stayed until nine o'clock pounding out emails on the red items to various departments around the company. In each one, she introduced herself, summarized the issue at hand, and listed numbered action steps, the person responsible for each one, and the specific time frame for the needed response. She offered to quickly reply to all questions and concerns, and copied Paul on every email. She got into a zone and the thought of food didn't cross her mind until she got home. Then it was ramen, grapes, and a shower before flopping into bed.

Thursday morning, she returned to the office before Paul, straightened his desk again, and dived back into the emails. Paul arrived later with a slice of cinnamon crumb coffee cake. "Lori made this yesterday. With the new baby coming soon, she's gotten really into baking. I read your emails after the kids were asleep. First class work—clear and direct. Here's a tip—don't copy me on emails. When you do, people send their questions to me and ignore you. Just give me a daily status report and let me know when you run into problems you can't solve."

"Should I be copying Jack?"

"Definitely not! He's not an email guy and just gets annoyed. Leave Jack to me."

Cheryl smiled to herself as she took a bite of the coffee cake. Paul noticed her hard work. *I can do this!*

She finished the remaining red items and got going on the oranges. Over the course of the day, she began to see how SDI really worked. Like Rick warned her, *Reply All* was a disease.

Last night she emailed the main graphic designer for the Mega Motors account to remind him that the final layouts of the print pieces for the upcoming dealer meeting were overdue. This morning, a long list of new emails appeared in her inbox, with copies to Paul, from people she hadn't heard of. They went back and forth about the color scheme for the print pieces. One wanted to revisit a decision made weeks earlier: *I still believe that blue is a mistake for this client. Can we meet to review this before we commit to final?* The next one said, *We already made this decision.* The next three proposed possible times for the meeting and were quickly followed by various schedule conflicts that these unknown people had. Then Paul weighed in to remind them that the time for color scheme revisions had passed. He ended with *The next email to Cheryl and me should have the final layouts attached.* One of the unknown responders, apparently a graphic designer, complained: *If this company wants to maintain its reputation for excellence, design decisions should be made by designers, not by project management!!!*

Cheryl made good progress on her to-do list, even though she lost a chunk of time when Mavis invited her to a meeting about logistics for the SkyBridge new product launch tour. Cheryl didn't want to stop what she was doing, but was reluctant to say no and assumed that Mavis knew more than she did. Eight people sat around a table talking endlessly about issues that she didn't understand. Her anxiety rose as she sat there with nothing to contribute. In two hours, the group made three small decisions. Mavis, who invited Cheryl as a courtesy, saw her stone-faced discomfort and apologized afterwards. "I wanted you to see what we do, but you didn't need to be there. My bad."

At the end of the day, she met with Paul again to give him the status update. He was pleased by her progress and breathed a little easier—the hole he was in wasn't as deep as it had been a few days ago. He told her to plan to come in early the following Tuesday. "We're doing a Sprint for the Neighborly Mutual agents."

"What's a Sprint?"

"Sprint for the Spoils. Agents who beat their sales goals get to run through the SDI warehouse and grab as many items as they can. Every Sprint is a hoot. You'll love it. And Jack will be there. I told him about the great job you're doing and he's eager to meet you."

By late Friday afternoon, Cheryl was wearing down. She'd cranked out more emails, followed up with phone calls, and visited various departments to talk to people in person. All in an effort to push tasks through the innards of SDI. But it was slow going. Too many of her red items still couldn't be crossed off. She stared blankly at her computer display. *Nothing left to do today.* She packed up her stuff, walked towards the elevator and pressed the button. While she waited, she looked out a window to the parking lot. It was practically empty. Most people had gone home She wasn't looking forward to the long trek around the back of the warehouse to her Prius. As she stepped into the elevator, she had an idea. Instead of going to street level, she selected the lower level.

A few minutes later, after the *SDI YAH!* app guided her through a tangle of tunnels, she went up another elevator and emerged into Final Sound. She peeked through the glass door and Jeremy was there! He was flipping switches and twirling knobs. She opened the door to hear a crescendo of music and a silky female narrator. Jeremy swiveled around in his chair and broke into a wide grin when he saw her. His T-shirt read *Ask Me About Shamanism.* "Hey, Cheryl! To what do I owe the pleasure?"

"It's been a long, long week. I'm wiped. I need something to clear out my brain before I head home."

Jeremy arched his eyebrows. "A little pick-me-up? The pause that refreshes?"

Cheryl didn't understand what he was saying—and would have been shocked if she had. "If you're not leaving now, I was hoping I could listen to your sound system again."

"You bet! I've got miles to go before I sleep. Step into the preview room while I get something ready for you."

Cheryl sat down on one of the leather sofas. Jeremy's voice came over the intercom. "I want to play you a piece that really shows you what these speakers can do. Nothing like that client dreck you heard last time."

"What is it?"

"I'll tell you later. For now, just enjoy. As a bonus, there will be a little light show on the screen. A buddy of mine and I cooked it up."

The languid, liquid wail of a clarinet swirled above her, like the world waking from a long sleep. A gentle piano tiptoed to echo the horn's seductive spirit. Then, suddenly, the full thrust of an orchestra pressed Cheryl deep into the soft leather. The piano and the orchestra danced and pranced from enticing delicacy to delirious strength, lifting her into the heavens. With her eyes closed, her mind spun a universe of crowded streets, craggy mountains, and deep jungles. With her eyes open, lights squiggled and shimmered across the screen, with faint, fading glows trailing behind. Some moments inspired her with their majesty, others made her giggle with their silliness. Her cubicle, her computer, and the *Reply All* messages shrank to pinpoints and vanished in wisps of pink smoke.

When the music ended, after who knows how long, Cheryl lay limp on the sofa. Her ears throbbed in the unfamiliar silence. She blinked as she emerged from her magical trance. The lights came up and Jeremy entered, grinning from ear to ear.

"What was THAT?" she asked.

"Can you believe it's over a hundred years old?"

"You're kidding me."

"Nineteen twenty-four. George Gershwin. *Rhapsody in Blue.* The kind of music these little puppies were made for." He lovingly patted the ribbon speakers.

"Well?" Amy said over her cup of latte, with a mischievous smirk. "How did you survive your first week in the belly of the beast?" She and Cheryl were at their usual table in their favorite Saturday morning café on South Grand.

"Mixed. The work will be fine, nothing I can't handle, but the place is weird as hell." Cheryl described the labyrinth of offices, the massive warehouse, the high tech media production facilities, the video screens on every floor, and the company apps that talked to her through the earbud that HR said she was supposed to wear all the time,

"What kind of people work there?"

"Plenty of nutcases, but I also met a few who were pretty nice." She told Amy about the mystery man—her boss's boss, some kind of super salesman, who was out of town all week. "Everyone gave me an odd look or comment when I said I worked on his team."

"Did they put you in a cubicle?"

"Yes."

"Do you have a stapler?"

"Uhm, yeah."

"Don't let anyone take it!" Amy joked. Cheryl looked confused. "Haven't you ever seen the movie *Office Space*?"

"No."

"We'll watch it sometime. You can tell me how realistic it is."

Cheryl smiled. Amy was the one person she could relax with. Every Saturday morning with her was a refreshing tonic.

Cheryl spent the rest of the day cleaning her apartment, a Saturday ritual which was a sacred commitment. When she had been fired from the plumbing company, she was so depressed she holed up in her apartment for a week. The first two days, she cleaned every inch of it four times, from top to bottom. Then she caught herself and stopped. She fought the urge to keep cleaning because she didn't want to give her mother, Louise, the satisfaction of being right. Despite everything her mother had ever said about her, Cheryl knew that she was not OCD—a condition Louise learned about only from watching Dr. Phil's show on TV. Cheryl decided that cleaning only one day a week, even if for hours nonstop, didn't count as OCD. Making this compromise with herself—and sticking to it—became the first step in regaining her confidence.

She hated dirt, clutter, and germs, and felt more secure when everything was in its place. Occasionally, well-meaning people tried to entice her away with Saturday invitations to birthday parties, barbecues, or camping trips, but Cheryl learned it just wasn't worth it. The few times she had succumbed and skipped Saturday cleaning during the three years she had lived in the apartment she was dogged by anxiety until she made time to catch up. Changing the cleaning day to Sunday was a compromise that she had to make now and then, but it left her feeling uncomfortable for the entire week that followed. Moving it felt like a slippery slope that might work for other people, but not for Cheryl.

Her ritual had two parts. First, she vacuumed, dusted, and mopped the entire apartment, then did one of her special deep clean routines. There were four of these and she rotated through them on a strict schedule. Today's special routine was the baseboards, which were magnets for dust, grit, and grime. She slid the furniture—sofa, bed, and dresser—away from the walls, vacuumed and mopped the floor, then got on her hands and knees to wipe the baseboards clean of dust and fuzz with cleanser and a wash cloth. The cleaning routine saved her sanity during the months between getting fired by the plumbing contractor and landing the SDI job, a time when she had almost fallen into the abyss. It was a relief to continue the rotation now when her anxiety was receding.

While she worked, she listened to the latest episode of Annabelle Sinkovsky's podcast, *Illusions and Delusions*. This week's show covered the recent advances in green construction and net zero energy buildings. It was clear and persuasive, like all of Annabelle's talks.

The solutions and the technologies are right here, waiting for us to use them. Nothing new has to be invented. They don't deprive us of comfort; they make our homes more comfortable. They don't cost us; they save us money over the life of our homes. So I ask you, what are we waiting for? What are governments waiting for? What are building codes waiting for? What are banks and lenders waiting for? I urge you, my listeners, to force them to answer this question: What are you waiting for?

Annabelle was the founder and president of the Climate Crisis Coordinating Committee and Cheryl's number one climate hero. Her photo was taped to Cheryl's refrigerator. Not just any photo—Annabelle's iconic *People* magazine cover, which proclaimed her *The Fearless Voice for the Planet*. Cheryl had followed Annabelle's rise to the pinnacle of the environmental movement, from the publication of her first book, also titled *Illusions and Delusions*, through her famous testimony to the Senate Science and Technology Committee, to her many TED talks. She fascinated Cheryl because she could speak the truths about climate change, without sugarcoating anything, in a way that made people listen. *Yes, she's got the long hair and the etched cheekbones of a movie star. But she knows the facts and isn't a pushover. She is out there fighting the good fight. And they love her.* Everything made sense when Annabelle explained it. She spoke the truth and connected the dots in a way that inspired people to take a stand against greed and stupidity. Cheryl wished she could be like that—confident, persuasive, and fearless. Instead, when she talked to people about the crisis, either she was ignored or she got sucked into nasty arguments that never changed anyone's mind. Like at the family Thanksgiving a few years ago at her parents' modest one-story ranch house in south St. Louis County. Before the meal, Cheryl's older brother Kevin was showing off his prized new possession, a shiny blue behemoth of a pickup truck with huge tires. Cheryl criticized it as a hideous, gas-guzzling monster that would destroy the planet. Kevin was incensed. "My truck is none of your goddamned business!" Soon they were screaming at each other in their parents' driveway. Louise pulled her away and whispered to her to leave Kevin alone. "That's his pride and joy." Cheryl was furious. "Does he care more about his stupid truck than about me? Is it more important than the future of the planet?" As the family gathered to watch the brouhaha, Cheryl unbuttoned her shirt to proudly reveal a tattoo on her shoulder with an image of the earth and *Save the Planet: 350 ppm/1.5°C*, which were the global goals of the climate campaign. "This is my present to myself this Christmas, so everyone will know what's at stake and what I stand for." As she explained what the numbers meant, family members drifted away and rolled their eyes. Cheryl was left standing alone, in tears, seething with both anger and self-recrimination.

She knew she had blown it and tried to apologize to Kevin the next day, but her calls went straight to voicemail and her texts weren't delivered. He had blocked her number. Her parents avoided talking with her. They were polite, but distant. That's when she realized the time to move out of their house had come.

As she scrubbed the baseboard, Cheryl hoped that if she listened and read enough, some of Annabelle's magic would rub off on her. When she finished, she went online to calculate how much her carbon footprint would increase with the daily commute to SDI. She planned to use some of her paycheck to buy an equivalent amount of carbon credits—a tiny, pathetic act, but better than nothing. Buying the offset would reduce the guilt pangs when she was driving to SDI every morning.

Sprint for the Spoils

After cleaning her apartment on Saturday, Cheryl decided to unwind on Sunday. She ignored a group text from the C4 coordinator about a potluck that afternoon. She felt a little guilty about skipping it, but knew she needed time alone to recharge. Next week at SDI was going to be plenty intense. Also, Amy was the only one of the volunteers who knew about Cheryl's new job and she didn't want to get into conversations with the others that might spill the beans about her sellout. She shopped for groceries at the organic food co-op for the first time in months. Though she was still technically broke until her first SDI paycheck came through, she felt she deserved the reward of fresh fruits and vegetables. She spent the rest of the day at home alone, in peace. To make up for missing the potluck, she caught up on her climate change news, reading the latest articles from the Intergovernmental Panel on Climate Change and the NASA Climate Change site. The facts and figures were always depressing, as they revealed humanity's relentless spiral into disaster. Still, Cheryl wanted to know the truth and couldn't stay away. In the evening, she unwound by indulging her weakness for true crime reality shows on TV, the sleazier the better, before falling into bed.

Monday was a good day. Paul was consumed with final preparations for tomorrow's Sprint for the Spoils and he gave Cheryl the assignment to prepare a detailed status report on all the active projects for the team meeting with Jack Weatherly scheduled for Wednesday. It was just the kind of task Cheryl liked—organizing disparate information into a clear, concise form. She looked forward to Jack's reaction to seeing her work for the first time. He was sure to be impressed.

Soon after she began, her earbud chirped. "Good morning, SDI family. Mr. M here. I want to wish you T-G-I-M! Thank God It's Monday! I promise to make the most of this fresh opportunity to walk the road of success, and I know you'll do the same. Together, we'll reach the promised land. And don't forget that your quarterly performance point totals will be posted at the end of business on Friday. Show me and the executive team what you're made of!"

All day long, she heard Paul's phone ring again and again. Jack was calling with a slew of questions and last-minute changes on the Sprint.

"You're gonna love this!" Paul and Cheryl entered the cavernous warehouse, which was transformed from the way it looked last week when Dougie revealed the view from the conference room window. Now a temporary bleacher had been erected along one wall and a giant banner fluttered above it, *Neighborly Mutual Sprint for the Spoils*. Red, white, and blue bunting hung from the ceiling. An oompah band, five guys in lederhosen and little porkpie hats with feathers, tooted out oldies tunes on tuba, trumpets, and accordion. Cheerleaders brandished pompoms and went through routines in front of the bleacher. Paul, who had to speak loudly over the music, explained that they were recruited from a nearby high school.

He described how the Sprint worked. The contestants were insurance agency salespeople who have beaten their targets for selling policies from Neighborly. Each "winner" ("Every chance we get, we remind them that only 'winners' get to be here.") is given three minutes to dash through the warehouse with their spouse ("We like to keep the families involved.") to snag as many of the best items they can. Afterwards, SDI adds up the point value of everything they put in their cart and they get credited with that amount of points to use for whatever they want from the catalog, and the client was billed for those points. He told her that he and his wife did a Sprint a few years ago and finished with enough points for a full dining room set. "She still talks about it!"

"Is Jack here?" Cheryl asked.

"Not yet, but any minute."

Big video screens were showing Neighborly Mutual commercials as the oompah band led a procession of contestants and their spouses to the front of the bleacher. The contestants were wearing gag outfits their agency friends had made up for them. Silly hats and Hawaiian shirts. Spectators—people from the local Neighborly offices plus SDI employees brought in to make the crowd look bigger—waved homemade signs and cheered. An SDI video crew recorded everything. An announcer, who Cheryl recognized as a local TV weathercaster, introduced each contestant when it was their turn to sprint. "Please give a big Neighborly welcome to Dave and Pam Emerson from Tri-County Insurance in Poughkeepsie, New York!

Dave has led his team in life, casualty, and auto policies for seven months in a row! This man can sell with the best and now he's a winner!" A bell rang and Dave and Pam were off. She grabbed Gucci purses while he swept boxed silverware sets into the cart. They dashed to the next shelves that were loaded with cameras and electronics. Dave, who was six-four, leaped up and snagged a Rolex off a top shelf. "Great move!" Paul whispered, "The client's budget estimate wasn't expecting that one." When the scoreboard clock counted down to zero, the buzzer went off, and Dave and Pam, sweating and breathing heavily, pushed their loaded cart back to the starting line, high fiving everyone around them while the warehouse people totaled up their haul and refreshed the items on the shelves. "This will go on for a couple hours," Paul said. The bell rang and the next pair of contestants started their sprint.

A man with a big grin appeared next to Paul and slapped him on the back. "How ya doing, my friend?"

"We're digging the Sprint," Paul said and pointed to Cheryl. "This is Cheryl Ricard, who I told you about. Cheryl, meet Jack Weatherly."

Jack grabbed her hand in both of his and looked her straight in the eye warmly. "Welcome to the team, Ricard! I'm so pleased to finally meet you. Even though he can't sing worth a damn, Paul sings your praises every day. He tells me we can really count on you…when we need a plumber!" Jack laughed at his own lame joke, which annoyed Cheryl. He didn't look anything like the Superman type that she had imagined from all of last week's comments. He was about fifty years old, average height and a little pudgy, with short, curly blond hair. Kind of forgettable, except for his piercing blue eyes. He talked with Cheryl like she was the only person in the warehouse.

"Don't you just love the Sprint? It's the heart of what Success Dynamics is all about." He gestured to the group of contestants. "These insurance agents deserve a moment in the sun and I'm proud as hell that we can provide it. Most of the time, their bosses lean on them to push harder on products their customers may not even want. I feel kind of sorry for them—no one grows up dreaming to sell insurance—but then life ain't fair. No one knows that better than a salesperson."

To Cheryl, watching the Sprint was a surreal spectacle, like something out of Monty Python, but Jack's concern for the plight of the contestants caused her to see it a little differently. His smooth, almost eloquent, voice made the noise and chaos less stressful for her. Then she noticed that he was suddenly distracted by something behind her. In mid-sentence, he said "Gotta go," and left abruptly. She turned around and saw him greet a man with the same intensity he had just been showering on her. They both began laughing about something.

"The client from Neighborly, James Chieng, just arrived," Paul said. "The first thing about Jack you need to understand is that, when a client is around, we don't count."

Cheryl watched more of the insanity of the Sprint and kept an eye on Jack as he yukked it up with the client. After the Sprint ended and the client left, Jack came over to Paul and Cheryl. "I love these Sprints. They always warm my soul. You'll get your chance to do one someday, Ricard. Paul, you make sure of that. Hey, can we move the team's meeting earlier tomorrow? To seven o'clock? I just set up a round of golf with Chieng before he leaves town. A few vultures are circling around our business. I need to nip that in the bud." Cheryl saw the pained expression on Paul's face as he said "Sure, Jack. No problem." He told Cheryl to alert the team members to the new time.

Jack had ordered a spread of bagels, muffins, and coffee from the SDI cafeteria. Paul, Cheryl, Mavis, Rick, and Mary Ann were all there, along with two other travel directors Cheryl had met briefly in the useless meeting the previous week. Jack was the last to arrive, wearing his golf outfit of a bright pullover shirt and crisply creased pants. "Good morning, team. Let's get it on!"

Paul handed out the status report that Cheryl had prepared and began going through it page by page. Jack listened, but didn't look at his copy. He stirred his coffee, put jam on his bagel and seemed impatient. Cheryl realized that he wasn't going to read the meticulous, well-organized report she worked for hours to create. He interrupted Paul's review. "You guys can figure out the details later. Something big is going on with every client. I want to start with that." He explained that competitors were sniffing around at Neighborly and that his golf game with Chieng would be the first step in locking the business down. SkyBridge, on the other hand, was an opportunity to expand. "They're considering adding travel rewards, my sources tell me. The client hasn't asked me for anything yet, but I want to surprise them with a proposal that blows them away so much that they won't even think of getting other bids. How's that coming?"

Mavis answered. "I'm working on it with the Global Experiences department. Vendor quotes are coming in, but it's slow. We're developing some outstanding, very original options."

"When will it be ready?"

"Three weeks, two if there aren't hiccups."

"Not good enough. I need it Monday."

"Impossible."

"Make it work. I have a meeting with the VP next week. I want to blow her away."

"We can't get the pricing right by then."

"You're a professional. You know what things cost. Give it your best estimate."

"That's very risky. If the numbers come in higher than we expect, we could lose our shirt."

"Hmm. I see your point, Mavis. What company do you work for?

"SDI."

"Why is SDI big and successful?"

"We deliver memorable, high-quality experiences."

"Bullshit! That's what you're supposed to say. Actually, SDI is big and successful because we get there first with a killer concept. Our biggest risk is not getting this piece of business at all. I don't need airtight numbers on a project that the competition takes away from us. I want to win the battle before the battle begins. Like that Chinese guy said. You know, what's his name—Susie Q."

"Sun Tsu" Cheryl said.

"Yeah, him. I want to put our pitch in front of the VP next week, before she even has a clue about what she wants. I'm gonna shape her thinking so we become her only choice. Dazzle her with our creativity."

Mavis was about to object when Jack looked right at her and said, "Monday, OK?" She reluctantly agreed. Her weekend was shot. As it was for Paul, Rick, Cheryl, and the Global Experiences department.

Jack said, "I'm running out of time. Let's move on to the big kahuna, the Mega Motors dealer meeting. We got three weeks to go."

Paul reviewed all the logistical plans and issues in Cheryl's status report. Everything was under control.

Jack poured himself a second cup of coffee. "We can't afford another screw-up like last year, when the awards plaques were full of typos." Actually, there had been only one typo, but as far as Jack was concerned, that was one too many.

"I'm on it, Jack." Paul insisted. "And I'll be at the meeting the whole time. Nothing will slip through."

"Let's mind our Ps and Qs. Mary Ann, how's the stage show coming?"

"Media is all done, ready for client review. Script is written. Performers are booked."

"The client just told me he doesn't want the auto babes this year."

"What? The whole show is built around them. What the hell are we supposed to do?"

"He says that he and the CEO have a new concept. I'll hear it on Friday."

Mary Ann was exasperated "There's no time!"

"I know you can pull off a miracle. You always do." Now, Mary Ann's weekend was also shot.

Jack looked at his watch. "Gotta go. Thanks, everybody."

On his way to the door, he said to Cheryl. "See, Ricard? We know how to have fun!"

After the team meeting ended, Cheryl had a question for Mary Ann. "What's an auto babe?"

"A showgirl. A dancer with long legs and a sexy outfit. They cavort around the stage at key points in the show, especially during the new car reveals. The dealers go apeshit over them."

Cheryl scrunched her face in disgust. "Gross."

"It's not as bad as it sounds. We've been using auto babes for years. The dealer guys ogle them, but that's about it. We hire showgirls from Vegas, who know how to take care of themselves."

"Are they prostitutes?"

Mary Ann laughed. "Hardly. They're in a union. Most are married with kids. Very no nonsense, despite whatever the dealers are dreaming about."

"So why aren't we using them this year?"

"Beats the hell out of me."

Mary Ann was resigned to the chaos to come. "Jack's default position is that we're all borderline incompetent and he has to save the day. But I gotta say one thing. He's tuned into every little ripple in the client's mood. And he's usually right about that."

"What will you do?"

"When the chips are down, he'll listen to reason. And he knows not to mess with me."

It was a long, hard weekend. Cheryl had to cancel her Saturday coffee with Amy and, with great anxiety, her cleaning routine. She and Paul were the first to arrive in the conference room Saturday morning. Cheryl dreaded spending the weekend stuck in this room. Working alone was so much less stressful—and it would be hard to shake the thought of the filth festering in her apartment. Paul explained that when top quality work needed to get done in a hurry, the SDI way was to gather a team in one room to work side by side until the job was finished. "You'll get to see how we do things when the stakes are high."

Soon the others arrived—Mavis, the two people from the Global Experiences department, and Rick, who was there to make the proposal look spectacular. Paul stood at the whiteboard and wrote the mission for the weekend. The others chimed in with questions or comments. Cheryl noticed that everyone got a chance to speak and no one was grandstanding. Mavis cracked joke after joke to smiles and chuckles. Paul was a quiet, but decisive, leader. Soon each person had a list of tasks for the day. Cheryl's first job was to assemble the messy scribbles on the whiteboard into the outline for the proposal—just the kind of thing she was good at. Rick patched his computer into the video screen on the wall. Everyone could see how he was organizing images and other design concepts into the pages of the proposal.

People mostly worked quietly. Every few hours, Paul called a pause so each person could update the team on their progress. If someone was stuck, he led a quick brainstorm to help them past the obstacle.

By Saturday evening, pizza boxes were scattered around the room as the proposal began to take shape. Cheryl had to type furiously to keep her notes and outline up with the torrent of ideas. She was surprised at how much was getting done so quickly. Paul took a break to tell bedtime stories to his twins over the phone. "If they don't have their stories, Lori will never get them to sleep."

The team worked past midnight on Saturday and reconvened Sunday morning for the final push. Jack came in Sunday afternoon to review the draft. The exhausted team members were on edge as they watched him read the proposal. How much more work was he going to throw at them? He was uncharacteristically quiet and made notes in the margins of his copy. He offered a few edits and asked questions. He called one page of the proposal "total crap" that would never fly with the SkyBridge client. It was the product of several hours of work.

Jack watched the video screen as Rick cut out the offending page. Paul said the team would put the finishing touches on tonight so the final proposal would be ready to go Monday morning. Jack looked at the title page, with Rick's striking design, one more time. Then he said, "I can sell this."

Later, Paul told Cheryl that, coming from Jack, these words were high praise.

They finished the proposal Sunday night. Paul told the team to sleep late and take their time before coming into the office tomorrow. Cheryl woke up extra early Monday morning to make up, at least a little, for the weekend cleaning she had missed.

On Monday, Paul told Cheryl he wanted her to analyze every detail of the planning for the Mega Motors meeting, a four-day long event with a thousand people. Nothing could be allowed to fall through the cracks. He knew Jack well enough to see he was on high alert. "He hates it if the client finds a mistake. And I get the sense that he's worried something weird is going on. When Jack says, "Let's mind our Ps and Qs," that means he suspects the client is nervous. Especially true with Mega this year. The main client contact is a new guy Jack doesn't know well."

"How can I analyze the plan when I don't know anything about dealer meetings?"

"Your inexperience could be an advantage. Look at the process with fresh eyes. You may see something that the rest of us missed."

As Cheryl stood up to leave his office, Paul gave her one last piece of advice. "Don't be shy about pushing for information. There's a fine line between nagging and negligence. Err on the side of nagging. I'd rather hear people whine that we're bugging them too much, than to hear from Jack or the client that we missed something."

Never in her life had she thought about a car dealer meeting, not even for a second, and now she found herself in the thick of one. She was surprised to see how many moving parts there were where any number of little things could go wrong, from the welcome gala to the catered meals, twenty-four hour open bars, audiovisual equipment rented for the multitude of breakout rooms, golf, tennis and horseback riding arrangements, elaborate technical requirements for the main event stage, performers and musical entertainment, and the infamous award plaques, with last year's disastrous typo.

After the intensity of the previous week, when Cheryl had to endure both the noise and chaos of the Sprint and the multi-day, pizza-fueled slog of the SkyBridge proposal, it felt soothing, almost luxurious, to work alone in her cubicle. She sat at her desk reviewing documents, sending emails, and making phone calls.

People from several SDI departments, as well as the hotel, event planning company, and more, were involved. Every time she turned over a rock, there was another SDI department or vendor underneath it. As Paul explained to her, they all were good at what they did, but problems popped up when handoffs didn't happen, when one person thought that somebody else was handling something, but that person didn't have it on their to-do list. Hundreds of balls were in the air and if one were dropped, Paul and Cheryl had to be there to catch it. Mega Motors was paying big money to SDI. They expected perfection and so did Jack.

As updates came in, she filled a whiteboard with task lists and diagrams. Mary Ann helped her understand the ins and outs of complex stage productions and Mavis gave her a quick review of travel planning. When needed, she brought two or three vendors and SDI team members onto the phone at the same time as she stepped through a task. She peppered them with persistent, probing questions:

"What has to be in place before you can start your work?"

"Do the people who do the task before yours know exactly what you need?"

"Who do you hand off to when you're done?"

"Does your plan align with the terms of the work order?"

"What have we overlooked?"

Cheryl was determined to leave nothing to chance. She prided herself on being a quick study. She had learned the plumbing business and its complex technical vocabulary in a few months, to the point where she could do everything but turn a wrench herself. Now she was doing the same with this dealer meeting. Paul checked in with her a few times and realized that the best thing he could do was to stay out of her way. She wanted to prove herself to him and also to Jack, who she was pretty sure didn't take her seriously.

Cheryl was on fire. She didn't have time to waste and she declined many requests for face-to-face meetings. It was much less stressful when she didn't have to deal with a room full of people. She read reports, compared statements of work, looked for mismatches and balls teetering on the edge of disaster. As she made progress, she added checkmarks to the flow diagram on her whiteboard—who did what, which tasks depended on the completion of other tasks, what was the critical path. She color-coded tasks by who was responsible for them—SDI, the hotel, caterers, the staging company, shippers, etc. Her flow diagram made the web of interdependencies clear—and also revealed a potential minefield. Any misstep could throw the project off course and upset both the client and—more critically for Cheryl and Paul—Jack Weatherly.

By late Thursday, almost every task, large and small, looked to be under control. Before going home, she opened one last email responding to her requests for information. It was from the designer for the welcome gift bags for each attendee. She clicked on the image he had attached. The design printed on each bag, *Mega Motors Dealer Extravaganza, El Dorado Hotel and Resort, Scottsdale, Arizona*, filled her screen. She stared at it. It didn't look quite right—something about the logo. She had first seen the Mega Motors logo on her tour of Final Sound, when Jeremy was editing a video for the meeting. *This one is different.* The intertwined M's were more rounded than the angular, sharp-edged letters in the video she had seen. She googled the Meta Motors website, which showed the same logo that Jeremy had used.

She called the designer, left a voicemail, then sent him an email that pointed out the discrepancy. He called back a few minutes later. "That design was approved!"

"By who? Send me the signoff sheet." He mumbled that he couldn't find it. Then he requested an in-person meeting with his manager and Cheryl for the next morning. Cheryl went to Paul, who was about to leave for home. He agreed that the bags had to be fixed. He offered to go to the meeting with her. Cheryl insisted she could handle it herself.

At the meeting the next morning, the designer and his manager were sitting next to each other at a conference room table. Cheryl spread the bag design on the table. The manager showed her the gift bag design from the previous year "See, same logo. What's the problem?"

"Mega changed its logo." She showed him the new Mega Motors logo from their website.

"No one told us. And your predecessor approved the design."

"My predecessor? The one who quit? Where's her signature?"

"My guy told you. We can't find it."

"Reprint the bags now!"

"Impossible. The rush charges will kill us. Can we bill the client with a supplemental?"

"To fix your mistake? No!"

The manager leaned back in his chair and folded his arms. "I'm not taking the fall for this." Cheryl was getting steamed. "Reprint the goddamned bags!"

"Don't talk to me like that! I've been doing this for twelve years. You haven't worked here for even a month!"

"All your experience hasn't stopped you from screwing up big time!" Cheryl realized that she was getting dangerously close to one of the tirades that had caused her so much trouble with her family and at the plumbing company. She really wanted to chew this pompous fool out, but knew it wouldn't be a good idea. She didn't need a bad reputation at SDI. She closed her eyes and took five deep breaths, the way Dr. Pettus had taught her back in high school. The designer and his manager stared at her and glanced at each other, confused.

"You're right. It will be expensive to reprint the bags. Someone could get in trouble for it. I have a better idea." She took out her phone. "Let's call Jack Weatherly, and see how he wants to handle this." A terrified expression came over the manager's face. He hemmed and hawed. "On second thought, let me talk to the vendor to see what options we have. No need to bother Weatherly."

"Get back to me by the end of the day with your plan in writing, a sample of the new bag, and an ironclad guarantee that a thousand bags will be delivered to the hotel two days before the meeting starts."

Cheryl had pulled it off. She was figuring out how to play company politics. It felt pretty good.

CLEANING UP

AFTER HER SUCCESSFUL WEEK scouring the Mega Motors project for mistakes, landmines, and screw-ups, Cheryl was ready to unwind. She met Amy to resume their Saturday morning coffee tradition. Cheryl's first SDI paycheck was in her bank account, so she insisted on treating Amy to the café's famous lemon ricotta pancakes. "Thanks for putting up with me through these dark months."

"No problem. And now I've got a friend who's rich." They clanked their coffee cups in a toast. "So what's the latest from Bizarro World?"

Cheryl told her about the Sprint. "It's like *Treasure Trove,* that quiz show we watched as kids, with the craziness dialed up to eleven."

Amy laughed her head off. "An oompah band? Cheerleaders? Thing should be called *Greed Gone Wild!* And did you meet the super salesman?"

"I did. He doesn't look like much, kind of a schlub. He makes terrible jokes and is very full of himself. Hard to see what all the fuss was about." Cheryl recounted her efforts to analyze the dealer meeting. "It's amazing how much work they put into something that normal people don't even think about."

"What would you know about what normal people think?"

"Ha ha. Touché." Cheryl loved Amy, who knew how to gently rib her without making her feel anxious. Cheryl told her the story of her best moment so far at SDI—the confrontation over the gift bags with the wrong logo. "The guy tried to pull rank on me. I wanted to ream him out so bad, but I came up with a better way. Turns out that he was afraid of Jack, just like the rest of them."

"In honor of your triumph, come over to my place for Thai carryout this evening. We'll watch *Office Space*. Maybe we can hit a club or two afterwards."

Amy knew better than to suggest doing anything on a Saturday afternoon.

Cheryl had missed the previous Saturday because of the long weekend on the SkyBridge proposal, so today she would complete two of her deep cleaning routines. She had also missed last week's episode of Annabelle's podcast, so she could listen to two episodes while she worked. The first deep clean focused on her clothes. She emptied dresser drawers, wiped inside each one, then folded and restacked her clothes neatly. Next, she did the same with her closet, organizing outfits by color and experimenting to find the best strategy for placing the new pieces Amy had picked out for her to wear at SDI. As she worked, she listened to Annabelle, even though the subject was depressing— the relentless drumbeat of heat, drought, storms, and fires from all over the world.

News we all knew was coming, but which we hoped was still off in the distant future. Well, I'm sad to say, the future is now.

Cheryl laughed. It was the same as the tagline from the Mega Motors video she watched Jeremy edit. She knew that it meant something very different when spoken by Annabelle.

The time for wishful thinking is over. The only way forward to slow down the climate disaster is to apply focused action, based on rigorous research. To challenge assumptions, zero in on solutions that will really make a difference. We can't just wish climate change away or cling to feel-good policies that won't get us anywhere. We must work harder, my friends, and I promise you that everyone at C4 will do our part.

Annabelle's words always gave Cheryl hope and new ideas. Yes, the situation in the world was dire, but maybe there was still a path forward.

She got out her supplies for the second routine for the day, mold removal. The apartment was in a hundred-year-old building which had not been maintained well—which was why the rent was cheap enough for Cheryl to afford—so mold was a frightening, insidious threat. Black smudges could spread silently wherever moisture lingered. She knew that mold would swallow up the apartment and infiltrate her lungs unless she kept it at bay.

Cheryl had a long and complicated history with mold. She learned about its danger at an early age. Growing up, she had to help her mother scrub tile surfaces and crevices in the kitchen and bathrooms with bleach solution, sponges, and brushes for the narrow places. Louise made Cheryl work for hours at her side, when all Cheryl wanted to do was to be in her room to soothe the feelings of her dolls, who were always quarreling about something or other. Young Cheryl took great pride in her ability to bring harmony to the society of dolls. Her brothers were exempt from mold removal duties and most other household chores. They spent their Saturdays in the back yard building forts out of patio furniture and playing touch football. Despite her resentment, Cheryl came to love the heady, comforting aroma of bleach as she scrubbed. It brought her a calming sense of order.

When she became an environmentalist, she learned about the harmful impacts of bleach on ecosystems and faced a dilemma. How could she protect herself from mold without compromising her principles? There were two schools of thought about the best cleanser for mold: bleach vs. vinegar. She made the difficult decision to switch to vinegar for her monthly mold routine. She explained the hazards of bleach and the safer alternative of vinegar to her mother, who brushed off her concern. Louise was not about to give up her bleach. No way. This was Cheryl's first lesson in the limits of logic to convince people to make environmentally responsible choices. Old habits were hard to overcome.

Now Cheryl broke with her mother every month on mold Saturday, when she filled a spray bottle with a four-percent vinegar solution. She put on an N95 mask and used a rag and old toothbrush to scour every corner and crevice of the apartment where mold could find a foothold. It felt good to be charting her own path in life, though she missed the guilty pleasure of bleach aroma. She began at the kitchen sink, scrubbing every inch of the surface, then emptying and cleaning the cabinet underneath. After the kitchen, she moved to the main field of battle, the bathroom and shower. She sprayed and scrubbed, scrubbed and sprayed. When she did her mold routine, the apartment smelled clean and fresh in a way that reassured her and created a satisfying conclusion to the day. Vinegar didn't bring back her childhood, but it was now almost as satisfying to her as bleach had been long ago. Even when it was cold outside, she opened the windows to let in a fresh breeze. Cool air enhanced the bracing aroma of vinegar.

Annabelle's second podcast was the perfect soundtrack to Cheryl's campaign against mold. It was entitled *Are You A Climate Warrior?*

Often, we have to compromise—to accept a partial solution, even when we know it doesn't do enough. A climate warrior compromises when nothing else is possible. Half a loaf is better than none, but a climate warrior doesn't rest afterwards. Each partial victory becomes the foundation for the next struggle. Climate warriors may compromise, but we never rest.

Climate warriors listen to other points of view, but we always speak the truth.

Climate warriors are fearless, but we seek to understand those who fear change.

Climate warriors follow science as the guide to meaningful action. Not easy solutions, but real ones.

Climate warriors are happy because we are fighting for everyone. We are inspired by the beauty of the natural world, the gentle caress of a soft puff of wind, the flitter of butterflies, and the colors of a wildflower meadow.

What inspires those who stoke the fossil fuel fires? Those who are driven by greed to ignore the ugliness and destruction? No matter what they say about us, we climate warriors can hold our heads high.

Annabelle's uplifting words blended with the aroma of vinegar to make Cheryl's afternoon perfect. She sat at her kitchen table and wrote a check for the carbon credits to offset her commute to SDI.

Watching the movie *Office Space* at Amy's was a hoot. It nailed the weirdness of cubicle life perfectly.

Amy said, "Here's my big question, are you Milton?"

Cheryl gave her the side eye look, then broke out laughing.

"I'm serious," said Amy. "What's the female version of Milton? Miltina? I'm going to start calling you Miltina!"

Soon they were both laughing hysterically. Cheryl didn't know what she would do without Amy.

Peace and Quiet

Cheryl had her easiest week yet at SDI. She wheeled her whiteboard into Paul's office to review the results of the previous week's troubleshooting exercise on the Mega Motors meeting. She led him through her findings and answered all his questions. Paul was extremely appreciative, especially about her discovery of the error on the gift bags. "That would have sent Jack through the roof!" Paul planned to travel to Scottsdale next week to be on site for the duration, "Over the years, I've learned to expect surprises at these meetings. I can almost guarantee you that something will go wrong. And Jack will be on high alert for the faintest sign that the client or a dealer is unhappy. You think my phone rings a lot now? It'll be nonstop out there."

As he and Cheryl were going over a few final items he wanted her to work on, his phone rang. "Hey, Jack. What do you need?"

Back in her cubicle, Cheryl made a list of what she still had to do. It was pretty short, a welcome change from both the previous week and, she anticipated, from the week to come, when she would stay in the office to be on standby to help Paul with any issues that arose at the meeting. She got a call from Mary Ann, who invited her to meet for lunch in the cafeteria. Now that her first paycheck had come through, Cheryl felt comfortable skipping the sandwich at her desk and splurging on the cafeteria meal, which turned out to be both good and inexpensive. "They subsidize this place," Mary Ann said while they went through the checkout line, "They'd rather do that than have people drive off-campus for lunch and take a long time before coming back—which would be bad for productivity." Cheryl chose a tofu stir fry and Mary Ann a soup and salad combo. "Be sure to try the brownies—they're outstanding."

As the producer of the main stage events for Mega Motors, Mary Ann was also going to Scottsdale. "The new client, some bozo named Vincent Maranga, keeps changing his mind. I haven't met him yet, but every indication is that he's an idiot. I see a clusterfuck a-brewing. You're lucky you'll be out of the line of fire." They made small talk for a while. Mary Ann asked Cheryl what she did in her spare time. "I read a lot and volunteer with an environmental group called C4. Sometimes I go to dance clubs with friends."

Mary Ann had heard of C4, but didn't know much about it. "It's good that you have that to focus on, so this place doesn't become your whole life." Mary Ann described her passion in life—theater. She acted with a local amateur group. "I played Maggie in *Cat on a Hot Tin Roof* last year. I was a little too old, but I pulled it off. Got a half decent review in the paper. Williams creates female characters like no one else. He gives you so much to work with. Next spring I'm doing Blanche in *Streetcar.*"

She told Cheryl that she had spent a couple years in New York when she was fresh out of college "I had the usual dream of making it as an actor."

"What happened?"

"I found out how steeply the odds are stacked against you. It's brutal. You get worn out by the rejections and being flat broke all the time. Not to mention getting constantly hit on by jerks. So now this place is my profession, sad as that may sound, and acting is just my hobby." She asked Cheryl if she was in a relationship.

"I've had a few boyfriends, but no one right now."

"Remember, it takes a mighty good boyfriend to be better than none. I've learned that the hard way."

Cheryl laughed, "You got that right." Mary Ann was like the wise big sister Cheryl had always wished for.

With the more relaxed pace of the week, Cheryl felt ready to get back involved with C4, after making no commitments since she began her new job. She and Amy went together to a volunteer meeting, held at a local library, where the usual group of about a dozen people attended. Half were baby boomers who had been activists for years and all seemed to know each other. The rest were a mixed bag of younger people. Some, like Cheryl and Amy, were reliable. Others came and went. They talked big, but didn't follow through much—too busy camping and kayaking to show up at rallies and volunteer work days.

Nate, the local C4 coordinator, a soft-spoken, bearded man with a clipboard, ran the meeting. He thanked everyone who had come to the recent demonstration at City Hall to demand stronger carbon reduction goals. "Great work! We were on the ten o'clock news." One of the older people, a short, balding, white-haired man named Victor, remarked, "That was nothing. We should occupy the mayor's office and force the cops to carry us out. That would make some great TV!"

Someone else countered. "Easy for you to say. But some of us have jobs we don't want to lose."

After a few minutes of back and forth discussion, Nate called a halt. "An occupation is an interesting idea, but it could hurt as much as it could help. C4's strategy is persuasion and building a broad-based coalition. Let's focus on that."

"We didn't stop the Vietnam war by being polite," Victor huffed. "We put our goddamn bodies on the line! Direct action is the way to win!"

Nate ignored Victor's rant, which he had heard many times before, and went on to outline two opportunities for the coming month, manning booths at Saturday morning farmers markets around town and phone banking for C4-endorsed candidates in the upcoming election. Victor sulked with his arms folded on his chest. Cheryl and Amy volunteered for one of the farmers' market booths. All they had to do was hand out literature and ask people to sign petitions. Cheryl normally shied away from interacting with strangers, but felt she could do it if Amy were there. They were going to spend Saturday mornings together anyway. Even though phone banking could be done from home, Cheryl took a pass on that one. She had tried it once before, but got frustrated. Most people didn't answer and most of those who did quickly hung up after she started her pitch. In three hours, she had a handful of short conversations, all with people who said they already planned to vote for the candidate she supported. Phone banking wasn't for her.

As the meeting wore on, Cheryl found her mind wandering to thoughts of SDI, everything from Dougie's bizarre rant about rewards, to the crazy spectacle of the Sprint, to the satisfaction of finding the mistake with the gift bags, and standing up to the manager who didn't want to fix it. The best memories were her new friendship with Mary Ann and Jeremy's introduction to the thrill of

Final Sound. She knew that SDI was all about greed and ignoring the real needs of the planet—the exact opposite of the noble cause that C4 was fighting for—but it sparked a fascination and curiosity that lingered with her.

"I have some big news," Nate said as the meeting wrapped up. "Annabelle is doing a national speaking tour to promote her new book. There will be a speech here next month, though we don't know the exact date yet. I'll update you when the plans are more solid."

Cheryl was relieved that no one asked her what she was doing, so she didn't have to say anything about her new job.

At the end of her slow-paced week, she sneaked off to Final Sound for an immersive plunge into more of Jeremy's music. He welcomed her with his usual big smile. His T-shirt of the day read *And Your Little Dog Too*. Cheryl made a request.

"I need to get launched into the weekend. Got anything for that?"

He stroked his chin to mime deep thinking. "How about we go…exotic?" He led her to the preview room. She settled into one of the leather sofas as he dimmed the lights. She was transported once again. Rapid drumming with fingers, like tapping on a table faster than she could imagine anyone could do. Punctuated by a gently whining accordion and occasional shouts of joy. At first, Cheryl cringed—it felt jittery, not soothing. Then after a couple minutes, she surrendered to the layers of rhythms on top of rhythms which lifted her into a wordless paradise.

Afterwards, when she asked what the music was, he said. "We made history today. This is probably the first time that Indian music, the real thing, not the homogenized pablum for white people, has been heard inside the hallowed halls of SDI. That was my man, Zakir Hussain, the master of the tabla!"

Glorious weather held court at the Tower Grove Park farmers' market Saturday morning. The sun was shining, the late fall air was brisk, and the changing leaves of the tall trees paraded in their full brilliance. Cheryl and Amy sat at a table beneath a C4 banner with pamphlets and copies of Annabelle's book fanned out in front of them. They chatted, drank coffee, and bantered with the shoppers who passed by. Amy was a natural at starting conversations, collecting signatures on petitions, and selling the book. Cheryl enjoyed watching her cheerful confidence, which rubbed off on her. After Amy left to get more coffee, Cheryl began a conversation with a young mother, who carried a sleeping baby in a sling, about the best home renovation strategies for saving energy. While they were talking, the woman's four-year-old son peeked over the table in front of Cheryl. When Cheryl glanced down at him, he ducked below the table, only to inch his head up again, this time with an impish smile. Cheryl looked at him with an exaggerated stern expression and he ducked again. "He'll play peek-a-boo for hours if you let him," the mother said.

"Hey, I have a present for you, but only if I can see you," Cheryl said to the little boy. He stood up straight and grinned expectantly. With a show of great ceremony, she handed him a copy of C4's coloring book for kids. "I know you're going to draw some beautiful pictures." He clutched it to his chest. The mother said, "What do you say to the nice lady?" He mumbled a thank you. As the little boy walked away, holding his mother's hand, he turned back to Cheryl and blew her a kiss. That little kiss melted her heart. For the first time in her life, the idea of having children appealed to her. She was surprised that the image of a sweet child holding her hand lodged so comfortably in her mind. Just as surprising, she was thinking about a future that wasn't defined by the onrushing climate apocalypse.

"Excuse me. I have a question." A voice startled Cheryl out of her reverie. An older man stood in front of her. "What is a good source of information about sea level rise?"

She flipped back to her default mode—sharing her encyclopedic knowledge of climate change statistics.

That afternoon, Cheryl was back in her apartment, cleaning. This week's special routine was the refrigerator. She emptied it out, removed all the shelves and drawers, then washed them with hot water and organic cleanser. She wiped the interior walls down. The final step was to carefully check all the food, wipe jars and cans (she didn't use plastic containers), throw away anything that looked suspicious, and replace the rest into organized rows. The freezer required a different approach. Because water and cleanser tended to freeze inside, she cleaned with only a slightly damp cloth. Annabelle's podcast this week was about the false promise of carbon capture.

These startup companies all claim to have technology to suck carbon dioxide out of the air and reverse climate change. Every one of them is peddling a mirage. Even if they succeeded, the scale would be pitifully small, less than a millionth of what would be needed. Why does carbon capture get so much attention? Because fossil fuel companies, who fund most of the projects, are throwing out distractions to keep us from demanding renewable energy solutions. I won't fall for it, C4 won't fall for it, and neither should you.

On Sunday, she did her weekly shopping at the food co-op, caught up on her climate change reading, and binged on a new true crime series. At ten o'clock, her phone rang as she was getting ready for bed. It was Paul. "Change of plans. Lori is going into labor, which we didn't expect for two or three more weeks. I need you to cover for me in Scottsdale. You'll leave first thing Tuesday and come back on Friday night. I've already asked Mavis to book your flights."

"Uhm…are you sure I'm the right person?"

"You know the project better than anyone."

"Is Jack okay with this?"

"He doesn't have a choice. And, yes, he's fine. I just got off the phone with him."

After the call ended, Cheryl was in shock. Ready or not, she was shipping out to the front line. Would she be doing battle with incompetence, with Mega Motors, or with Jack? Or maybe all of them?

Extravaganza

CHERYL'S FACE WAS PRESSED UP against the window as she watched the stately procession pass below. Miles and miles of tan desert dotted with dark clumps of scrub vegetation. Wrinkled hills and the twisting veins of dry riverbeds. This land was inhospitable, not suited for human habitation, nothing like the rivers, farms, and forests she had seen when the plane took off from St. Louis. *What were people thinking when they built a city out here? There's no water!* Cheryl had never been to the Southwest before, and this trip was going to be bad news for her carefully-managed carbon footprint. She didn't have the heart to do even a rough preliminary calculation. Buying a carbon offset for the flight would cost way more than she could afford—and would never be reimbursable under SDI's travel expense policy.

As the pilot announced the approach for landing, Cheryl saw the first few scattered houses in the desert, then a blinding flash that she thought was the sun glinting off water. It was a solar farm, as big as a good-sized lake. Acres of gray rectangles in orderly, satisfying, straight rows. Cheryl smiled to see that someone was doing right by the planet. She felt a twinge of satisfaction. Maybe the years of Annabelle and C4 sounding alarms about the climate catastrophe were actually making a difference. Then the city appeared. Thousands of houses were packed along the grid of curving streets, punctuated by trees and bright turquoise swimming pools. As the plane descended further, everything moved faster. Insect-like cars and trucks streamed along a highway. Suddenly a golf course, with pale fairways and lime-colored greens, swept by below. She saw a few golf carts and a golfer swinging a club. Finally, a swoop of concrete and a gentle bump as the plane touched down. The pilot's voice welcomed them to Phoenix.

Cheryl picked up her luggage from the carousel, then took an Uber to the El Dorado Resort and Hotel in Scottsdale. The cost of the Uber was about the same as she spent on two weeks' worth of groceries at the food co-op.

The car drove up a long driveway lined with palm trees and stopped in front of a stately arched entrance way framed with fountains. A young man in a uniform opened her door. "Welcome to the El Dorado." A smothering blast of midday heat enveloped her. The young man picked up Cheryl's suitcase and gestured for her to follow him through a revolving door into the spacious lobby. Cream-colored arches reached up to the distant ceiling. The temperature inside felt chilly, borderline frigid. Cheryl wondered about the carbon footprint of this gigantic air-conditioned room. People were sitting, talking, and having drinks at clusters of sofas between planters with ornamental palms and exotic flora. The young man led her to the long, polished-wood reception counter. A banner behind the counter read, *Welcome Mega Motors*. Cheryl noted with relief that the logo was correct. She got her room key from the desk clerk, along with a note from Mary Ann to join her in the main ballroom.

She followed the young man with her luggage into the elevator. On the fourth floor, he opened the door to a room larger than her entire apartment. He pulled back a curtain to reveal a picture window with a view of a bright blue swimming pool surrounded by a patio with umbrellas and reclining chairs. Palm trees and the intense green expanse of a golf course lay beyond. The young man showed her how to log onto the hotel Wi-Fi and operate the television. She wasn't sure why he was going on so long explaining things she could easily figure out on her own. After a few minutes, he left. Only later did she realize that he was expecting a tip. She was embarrassed to be so thoughtless to someone who was just trying to make a living. This was her first time staying in an upscale hotel, so she didn't know the etiquette. She sat on the king-size bed, which was another first for her, and called Jack to let him know she was here. "Glad you, made it, Ricard. So far, so good, I'm counting on you to steer this ship away from the icebergs."

"Mary Ann asked me to meet her in the main ballroom."

"Yeah, they're rehearsing the big show. I'm on the back nine with clients and will catch up with you after we finish."

A welcome gift bag—with the right logo—was propped next to the enormous pillows. Cheryl took out the contents to see what was there. A golf shirt that said *Mega Motors Dealer Extravaganza*, a matching ball cap, sunscreen, and a packet of golf balls and tees.

Rows of chairs filled the empty ballroom, which could hold more than a thousand people. A large temporary stage had been erected at the far end. Cheryl found Mary Ann next to a soundboard in the center of the room. She was directing technicians as they aimed lights that hung from a grid in the ceiling, while an SUV, a car, and a pickup truck slowly drove onto the stage. Several people milled around them, taking photos with cell phones and posing for each other. One young woman hopped onto the hood of a car and mugged seductively for a young man recording her with his phone. Mary Ann picked up a microphone. Her commanding voice boomed through the room. "Get off the vehicle. You can only be on a vehicle when I tell you to." The young woman gave Mary Ann a pouty look as she jumped down from the car. Mary Ann saw Cheryl and lit up in a smile. She pointed to a table at the side of the room. "Grab something to eat. I'll just be a few more minutes." Mary Ann went back to giving instructions to various technicians. The lights dimmed and a video began to play on a big screen above the stage. Cheryl recognized it as *The Future is Now*, the same one she had seen Jeremy editing a few weeks before, on her first tour of Final Sound. Mary Ann issued a few more directions about the path the vehicles needed to take as they drove onto the stage. "Don't get bunched up. And give me a tight spot on downstage left. That's where the MC will be standing when the video ends."

She sat down next to Cheryl, who asked. "Who are those people on the stage with phones?"

"The influencers." Mary Ann said with air quotes. "They're the new talent that our client, Vince, has added to the show to replace the auto babes. They're supposed to post about the meeting on social media the day of the event. Apparently, they all have big followings. Working with them is like herding cats."

The rehearsal continued. Mary Ann walked to the stage to talk with the influencers. From her gestures and body language, it looked to Cheryl like she was laying down the law to them about where on the stage they could and couldn't be. She raised her voice and Cheryl heard her say,

"I don't care if you have a billion followers! Stay behind the vehicles. Don't take one step in front of the vehicles. The whole point of the show is for the audience to see the new vehicles!"

A door opened at the back of the room and in walked Jack Weatherly and another man. Both were wearing golf clothes. Cheryl met them by the soundboard. Jack shook her hand, "Good to see you, Ricard." His face was flushed and his shirt was soaked with sweat.

"Let me introduce you to Vince Maranga from Mega. Vince, this is uhm…." Jack had forgotten her first name. "Cheryl" she said as she shook Vince's hand.

Jack recovered. "Cheryl Ricard. She's fantastic and you can count on her to keep this ship on course. No detail slips past Ricard. And she has the unenviable job of keeping me on the straight and narrow." Both Jack and Vince guffawed loudly. Cheryl didn't think it was one bit funny. "Ricard, can you order a pitcher of G&Ts for Vince and me? The sun was brutal out there on the course." Cheryl was puzzled. What was he asking for? Jack looked at her like she was a dolt. "Gin and tonics." Jack and Vince walked toward the stage. Cheryl found a hotel phone and called to have the drinks sent to the ballroom.

At the stage, Vince introduced Jack to the influencers as Mary Ann stood nearby. There was a lot of laughter and backslapping as the influencers gathered around Vince, who loved being the center of attention. A waiter brought a tray with the ice-cold G&Ts. Cheryl told him to put it on the table with the snacks. She walked to the stage, got Jack's attention, and pointed to the drinks. He was deep in conversation with Vince, Mary Ann, and the influencers. He kept the conversation going as he led Vince to the table and poured him a drink. He said something that got Vince to laugh again and they clinked their glasses. The influencers started interviewing anyone they could find—lighting technicians, stagehands, waiters. One put his phone in Mary Ann's face and she brushed him away. Another started towards Cheryl and she waved her off before she got close.

Cheryl didn't know what to do, so she sat in a chair and watched for a while. Everything was new and strange to her. A hand tapped her on the shoulder. She turned around. It was Jack, "I'm going to get a shower. See you at the reception. Five-thirty."

Cheryl confessed her fear about the reception to Mary Ann. "I don't do well in crowds. I get anxious." Mary Ann offered to join her so they could go into the reception together. Before Cheryl left home, Mary Ann had texted her to bring something suitable for a social evening.

When she met Mary Ann in the lobby, Cheryl was wearing her only cocktail dress, black and slinky with spaghetti straps. She had bought it at an upscale thrift shop for Cousin Bob's fortieth birthday celebration a few years ago and hadn't worn it since. As she and Mary Ann walked to the reception, Cheryl said, "I hope I can do this." Mary Ann gave her a reassuring pat on the arm. "I'll be close by the whole time." A hotel attendant held a door open as they passed onto a huge outdoor patio with a swimming pool on one side. An ornate Spanish style marble fountain burbled. Palm trees provided pockets of shade. Elegant formal plantings filled raised beds. The late afternoon sun cast a rosy glow on the distant mountains. A mariachi band strolled around. A few hundred guests were already there, though there was still room for many more. Most were middle-aged men wearing blazers, slacks, and open collared shirts. All were Mega Motors dealers. There was a smattering of women, wearing expensive dresses and abundant jewelry. Mary Ann explained that, because this meeting was a "working session," though one with plenty of recreational opportunities, and not a rewards trip, spouses weren't invited. The women were also owners of Mega Motors dealerships.

Waiters circulated with trays of hors d'oeuvres and drinks. People were greeting each other, chatting, and smiling. They looked completely relaxed and comfortable. Cheryl had never seen so many wealthy, self-satisfied people in one place. These were the ones she had long despised, who were wrecking the planet for money, without giving it a second thought. Her brother Kevin and his pickup truck were nothing compared to this bunch. And here she was helping them! A wave of guilt washed over her.

"Do you know any of the dealers?" she asked Mary Ann.

"Not really. I've been doing this for almost ten years, I've had drinks with a few of them, but they barely remember me and don't care who I am. We're just the help, Cheryl. The only SDI person they might know is Jack. He works this crowd like his life depends on it."

She pointed to a small group across the patio where Jack was entertaining rapt listeners. A burst of applause rang out behind Cheryl and Mary Ann. They turned to see a white-haired man with a deep tan and a radiant smile enter the patio. "Now, here's someone who they don't consider to be the help."

"Is that the guy from *Treasure Trove*?"

"Yes, indeed. Mr. Lance Meadows, in the flesh." Cheryl had grown up watching *Treasure Trove*, her mother's favorite quiz show, which played in the kitchen almost every evening while they made dinner. "My mom's greatest dream was to be on that show. She moped around the house for weeks when it was canceled. What's he doing here?"

"Lance has been the MC of the Mega meeting for several years. And he has a good business of making personal appearances at dealerships around the country. As far as the dealers are concerned, he's one of them, a member of the club. You'll meet him at the rehearsal tomorrow. You can take a selfie for your mother."

Cheryl noticed that she didn't see the influencers anywhere. "Vince didn't invite them tonight," Mary Ann said. "He wants them to be a surprise to the dealers at the new model reveal on Friday."

Cheryl and Mary Ann wandered over to the buffet line, where more substantial food was waiting. They filled their plates and found a table. As the sun set, the light on the mountains became even more beautiful. Jack came over with a drink in his hand. He looked Cheryl up and down and nodded approval. "You're looking good, Ricard. Be careful out there." He waved his arm across the assembled dealers. "This is what the selfless heroes of our armed forces would call a target-rich environment. There's money lying around everywhere for those who know how to find it. A thrilling sight to behold!" He raised his glass to Cheryl. "Paul asked you to watch out for mistakes and fix them before the client notices. You're doing a great job, so keep it up!"

Then he glanced around and gestured to both of them to lean in, so he could say something without being overheard, "I'm kind of worried about Vince Maranga. All he could talk about on the course today was those influencer kids. What are they like, Mary Ann?"

"A little unruly, but I can handle them."

"What does Lance think?"

"We'll find out tomorrow. He never pays attention to this meeting until he gets here. I doubt he read the script I sent him."

"Vince believes the influencers are going to transform the dealer meeting into something trendy and modern. He's been selling it hard to Walter Lydecker, the CEO. I like my clients happy, but not manic. This whole deal has the smell of something that could blow up in our faces. So I want both of you to keep a close eye on it."

Cheryl began the next morning by checking several meeting rooms where dealer breakout sessions were scheduled, on topics like inventory financing, selling extended warranties, and increasing service department revenue. Because Mega Motors people were leading these, Cheryl only had to make sure that the AV equipment was set up and ready to go. Then she went to the main ballroom to watch the rehearsal.

No one was there when she came in, except for a couple of technicians at the soundboard. She got a muffin and coffee from the buffet table, found a chair, and opened her laptop to look at email. A little while later, a group of the influencers arrived. They filled plates from the buffet and sat together a few rows away from Cheryl. They talked loudly with each other, but didn't seem to notice her, which was fine with her.

They compared notes about last night's club hopping around Scottsdale. Some complained about hangovers caused by too many unwise tequila shots. "You asked for it!" one said to general laughter. A young woman said, "I don't know about you jokers, but I'm not gonna blow all the money I'm making here on partying. When next week rolls around, I'll still be pretty broke." The laughs died out as the conversation turned to the challenges of the influencer business. They all had similar stories. The social media platforms paid like crap, so sponsorships from companies like Mega Motors were the only hope. The trick was to be a corporate shill without looking like one to your followers.

The rest of the influencers trickled in and joined the conversation. Cheryl paid close attention, without lifting her eyes from her laptop.

Mary Ann arrived at the ballroom, along with a tall, slightly disheveled man. She introduced him to Cheryl as Dan Parnell, a writer from SDI who had just come to Scottsdale on a redeye flight. "Dan's been writing Lance Meadows' Mega Motors speeches for years."

As Mary Ann went to talk to a technician, Dan said to Cheryl. "Between you and me, this is the stupidest goddamned thing I've ever been mixed up in."

"What do you mean?"

"The song and dance with these influencers. It'll never work."

Just then, Lance Meadows entered. He strolled grandly down the aisle, shaking hands with bewildered technicians, then greeted Mary Ann warmly. She introduced Cheryl to him, "Her mother was a big fan of *Treasure Trove*."

"My fans are always closest to my heart!" He moved to stand next to Cheryl. "What's your mother's name?"

"Louise."

He pointed to Cheryl's phone. "Let's make her a video." Cheryl held up her phone and selected the selfie camera. When the *Record* light came on, Lance's face lit up in a big smile as he put his arm around her shoulder. "Good morning, Louise! Lance Meadows here. I'm so thrilled to be working with your lovely daughter, Cheryl. Now, we're having some fun!" That was his catchphrase from *Treasure Trove*. The second Cheryl pressed *Stop*, Lance turned back to Mary Ann, who briefed him on the layout of the stage. Cheryl wondered what to do with the video. She hadn't talked to her mother in months.

Vince Maranga rushed in. "Sorry I'm late." Mary Ann introduced him to Lance, who he had never met in person. Vince showered him with effusive praise. Lance was warm and polite to the client who was paying his fee. Vince asked where Jack was. Mary Ann said he was taking care of something and would be there shortly.

"Before we start," Vince said, "I'd like to introduce you to the other stars of this production." Meadows looked puzzled—like Mary Ann predicted, he hadn't read the script yet so he didn't know anything about the influencers. Vince motioned for the influencers to come over, all ten of them, and they shook hands with Meadows. "These are the faces of Mega Motors' growing social media presence, across all the major platforms. They represent our future with a younger demographic. During the show, they'll be roaming the hall, talking to dealers. And of course, they'll be on stage with you for some jokes and, you know, loose banter. This is going to be the most connected meeting we've ever had!"

Now, Meadows was thoroughly confused. Mary Ann stepped in. "Let's do a walkthrough, Lance. Everyone has a copy of the script and it's also loaded into the teleprompter."

The walkthrough began with music and a collage of images from Mega Motors commercials. Meadows strode onto the stage from behind a curtain, waving to the nonexistent audience. Two of the influencers followed him, pretending to record everything with their phones. Meadows spoke his welcoming remarks off the teleprompter, followed by, "You're probably wondering what an old guy like me is doing out here with these kids…." He stopped abruptly. "I am NOT saying the words 'old guy.' Give me something else!"

Dan the writer shouted out, "What a big star like me is doing out here with these kids."

Meadows nodded, then said the line that way. He went on. "They're bringing the magic of Mega Motors to a new generation of customers. And today, we're all going to help them do that." As he continued, more of the influencers appeared on stage, moving back and forth and miming with their phones in a choreographed pattern. They pointed their phones at Lance, at each other, and at the imaginary audience. Lance glanced behind him nervously to see what was going on. Vince was watching from the floor with a huge grin. No one besides him and the influencers knew this routine was part of the plan.

Dan whispered to Cheryl "I feel like I'm watching a Christmas pageant in an insane asylum."

Lance read his next line, "Let's give a warm welcome to the new Mega vehicles that are going to set the internet on fire." Colored lights swept the stage as the three vehicles drove slowly out. The influencers swarmed all around them. Lance was confused and looked to Mary Ann for direction.

"This is when you banter with the influencers. The dialogue is in the script, but you can adlib to make it more natural."

He went up to an influencer sitting inside the pickup. "What do you like most about this new Stomper?"

"The rock-solid handling and the big-ass dash display."

Lance fist-bumped him and moved to another influencer, a young woman on the hood of the SUV. "I see you're a fan of the all-new Sorcerer Sport Utility Vehicle."

"You're damn straight. I go for the super comfy seats and the killer performance!"

Mary Ann's voice boomed out over the PA. "Never, ever say the word 'killer' when you're talking about a vehicle! Try again."

Lance repeated his line and the influencer said, "I go for the super comfy seats and the awesome performance!"

Then, Lance walked over to another young woman who was taking a video of the car. "Looks like the Scimitar Sport has your attention."

"It's a girl car for sure. Curves in all the right places." She shimmied seductively.

"What's your favorite feature?"

"Well, gramps, the paint job is soooo sexy …"

"Gramps? Hold it right there, honey. Stick to the script!" He turned to give Mary Ann an exasperated look.

"We'll work on the banter later. Let's do your monologue from the podium."

Lance walked to the podium at the far end of the stage and began reading off the teleprompter. Two of the influencers came around in front of the podium to shoot video of him while two others photobombed him from behind. They had just committed the cardinal sin of his world—blocking the audience's view of Lance Meadows. He stopped cold. "What the fuck is going on?" He threw down his script and stormed off the stage. He yelled to Vince and Mary Ann. "Get these morons away from me!"

Vince ran over to calm him down, but soon they were in a shouting match. Some of the influencers were recording the whole thing, until Mary Ann shooed them away.

Lance yelled. "These clowns have no business being on my stage!"

"It's not your stage!"

"Oh, yeah? See how your dealers like it without me. I quit!"

Lance turned his back on Vince, then marched out of the room. Vince started yelling at Mary Ann, "You and your clueless company are ruining my connected meeting. You better get off your ass and fix this—now! Where the hell is Weatherly?"

Cheryl called Jack, who, thankfully, answered. "We're having a major meltdown. Please get over here ASAP!"

Vince was still fuming when Jack rushed in. He demanded that Jack get Lance back in line, pronto. "Meadows isn't the star he thinks he is. I can snap my fingers and one of the influencers will take over as MC." Jack didn't bother telling him that getting rid of Lance would be a great way to start a dealer revolt.

"Give me a few minutes to find him and smooth this over. Lance and I go back a long way. Artists can be temperamental." Because Vince had unwisely been pumping up his connected meeting concept to the Mega Motors CEO, Jack knew that his job was on the line if it failed.

"I'll give you ten minutes, but I'm not paying him a penny more!"

Cheryl went with Jack to look for Lance. As they left the ballroom, she caught him up on what happened and said "I was listening to the influencers before the rehearsal. They're hungry and broke. For a little bit more money, I think they'll agree to whatever you want."

They found Lance in the lobby, talking on his phone. He was booking a flight back to LA. When he saw Jack, he yelled, "No fucking way am I sharing my stage with those twits!"

"Relax, Lance. They got a little over eager. We can keep them out of your way. Remember, these kids look up to you."

"I'm very close to getting a new show. I'm not going to blow the deal with the syndicator by popping up all over the internet with a bunch of idiots. What if they make me look like a fool?"

Jack reminded him of all the business SDI had thrown his way over the years. Also, he knew that Lance's supposed new quiz show gig was probably a bluff.

"No commitments until I talk to my agent," Lance insisted.

He got the agent on the phone and put him on speaker. The agent's first words boomed out, "There's nothing in the contract about social media rights. If you want social media, it'll cost you."

"How much?" asked Jack.

"Twenty K."

"Don't make me laugh! How about ten?"

"And we get to approve their posts before they go out."

"And no one gets anywhere near me on the stage," Lance added. "Or says words like gramps or old guy!"

They made the deal. Ten thousand dollars for the social media rights with a limit of one short interview per influencer and Jack's prior approval of the posts. Lance and his agent didn't want to take the time to review the posts themselves and they trusted Jack.

After Lance returned to the ballroom. Jack asked Cheryl. "You said those influencers were hungry. How much will it take to bring them on board?"

"I don't know. A thousand apiece?"

"I'll spread ten grand among the influencers, to be paid after I approve their posts. We'll call it an investment in their good behavior."

"Vince said he wouldn't pay a penny more."

"If I can't hide twenty thousand bucks in a supplemental invoice for this huge meeting, along with something extra for our trouble, then I don't deserve to be in this business."

Jack held open the door to the ballroom so Cheryl could walk through. "By the way, nice work, Ricard."

The influencers huddled around Jack as he explained the new deal. He made it clear they had to keep quiet about the payments, which were strictly between him and them. "Don't breathe a word to Vince." Heads nodded. Then he talked separately with Vince and Lance. He got them to shake hands. All was well. The rehearsal would continue after lunch.

As he left the ballroom, Jack said to Cheryl, "If there was ever a time for a G&T, this is it."

Stars

THE COFFEE SMELLED AS GOOD AS IT TASTED. Cheryl savored the aroma as she sat on her hotel room's king-size bed, with her laptop next to her and her files and papers spread out. This was the first time she had used one of those single-serving pod coffee makers and she was surprised at how much she liked the coffee. The fragrance reminded her of Saturday mornings at the café with Amy. She made a mental note to email Amy with a report on the surreal weirdness of this hotel crawling with car dealers. However good the coffee was, the obscene waste generated by the coffee maker repulsed her. Each cup left behind a plastic pod destined to last an eternity, first in a landfill, then crumbling into tiny bits to foul the ocean. Yet the pods looked so innocent in their neat stack on a silver tray, next to a bowl of fresh fruit, replenished every day, for the thoughtless convenience of rich, coddled Americans. This was the world that SDI was in the business of selling. Soft lives of plenty for the privileged and consequences for the planet be damned.

She knew she didn't deserve to be in this plush hotel room, which itself didn't deserve to exist. An entire family in a developing country could live comfortably in here. The cost of her four-night stay could feed them for a year. But she had to admit it felt soothing, with the thick carpet, faint hiss of air conditioning—another environmental disaster—and the view of palm trees and mountains against a crystal blue morning sky. Was she getting seduced by the little luxuries that the corporations dangled in front of people like her? The Mega dealers felt happily entitled to all this, even though, in the big picture, they too were insignificant cogs in the machine, just the same as Cheryl.

After yesterday's craziness at the rehearsal, she was in no hurry to leave her room. She needed a few hours alone. She would check on the various meeting rooms later this morning. With the Lance Meadows kerfuffle behind them, she figured Mary Ann could have a productive final rehearsal before tomorrow's show. The new model reveal and a slew of speeches were going to close out the official program of this meeting. So far, she hadn't received any messages about screw-ups or unhappy clients. One email did pop up while she sipped her coffee—from Paul, who wrote that his wife had delivered the baby, a little boy, after a long night of labor. Everybody was healthy. He asked how the meeting was going and she replied that everything was under control—both Jack and Vince were happy—so he didn't have to worry. *Spend the time with your family and I'll give you an update at the end of the day.* She made herself a second cup of very good, scandalously over-packaged coffee and nibbled some fruit. She felt her principles succumbing to comfort. The phone rang. It was Jack. *Oh no, what now?* Her restful morning was about to end.

"Hey, Ricard. What are you up to?"

"Catching up on paperwork."

"I want to thank you for all your help yesterday. And I was wondering, have you seen anything besides the hotel since you've been here?"

"No."

"You can't come all the way to Arizona without experiencing the great outdoors."

"I don't play golf, Jack."

"I know that. But you absolutely must see the desert up close. It's amazing! I'm going on an off-road adventure today with a bunch of dealers. Come with me."

"I've got a lot of work to do and I thought I should watch the rehearsal this afternoon."

"Screw it. Have a little fun. That's what these meetings are all about. We'll leave at ten and be back in time for dinner."

Cheryl's morning of blissful solitude was over. She had only known Jack for a short while, but one thing was certain—he wouldn't take no for an answer. But why would he invite her?

"Meet me in the lobby. Wear a hat and bring sun protection. Lunch is included. See ya!"

Cheryl didn't know it, but she was the only person Jack could think of to invite. He was supposed to go on this tour with Vince, who had backed out at the last minute, saying he had to attend an emergency meeting with the CEO. Vince didn't tell him what the meeting was about, which worried Jack. He didn't like it when something mysterious was going on with a client. Picking up on rumblings of power struggles and impending shakeups was a key skill in Jack's success. He tracked down one of his longtime Mega Motors contacts in the lobby—who didn't know about a CEO meeting today. He asked Jack to fill him in if he found out anything.

Jack needed a partner for the off-road excursion. It wouldn't look good for him to be the only one riding alone in a dune buggy. Quiet little Cheryl was his only option. So he decided to do something very rare—a good deed for someone who wasn't a client. *Why not?* Also, he was a little curious about her. She seemed like an odd duck, but she had given him a good tip about the influencers, which had helped him figure out a way to head off the crisis. *Maybe there's more to this drab girl than meets the eye.*

When Cheryl joined the group of dealers in the lobby for the tour of the desert, she felt the vibe of a middle school field trip. They all had on their Mega Motors golf shirts and hats. They were joking and laughing and didn't pay any attention to her when she arrived. She didn't wear the logoed golf shirt from her gift bag—she wouldn't be caught dead in it. She did bring the hat with the Mega Motors logo—it was the only one she had and she needed something if she was going to be in the sun all day. The tour guide, an athletic man with an *Off-Road Arizona* polo shirt, was checking off names on his clipboard. Cheryl wasn't on his list. She explained that Vince Maranga couldn't be there and she was taking his place with Jack Weatherly.

Jack was the last to arrive. They boarded a bus for the one-hour drive to the trailhead. Coolers were filled with water, soft drinks, and beer. Quickly, dealers were popping open beer cans. "We're in the desert. Have to stay hydrated!" one joked as he tossed cans of beer to his buddies. Jack asked Cheryl what she would like. She held up her metal water bottle, branded with the C4 logo. She wasn't about to use a disposable plastic bottle and add to the disgusting mountain of waste clogging the ocean.

At the trailhead, lunch was served in a big tent. The guide showed slides of the beauty of desert flora and fauna and explained the rules of the tour. "Stay in sight of the other vehicles and only get out when I call a stop. Watch where you step so you don't disturb fragile desert plants." Before the excursion started, Cheryl watched Jack schmoozing with the dealers. He made it look effortless as he traded jokes with one and moved smoothly to a serious conversation with another, about something that seemed to be deep and important. During the course of a few minutes, he managed to interact with each one of the sixteen dealers. He was working the room. Despite her disdain for his gladhanding and shameless flattery, she had to admit his performance was masterful.

The guide led the group to a line of white Utility Terrain Vehicles, which he said was the proper term for what most people called dune buggies. Each one sat two people and was topped with a canopy to provide shade. He pointed out the coolers with snacks and drinks mounted behind the seats. He opened one and held up a pint bottle of tequila. "You all have a little taste of Arizona's finest waiting for you. What happens in the desert stays in the desert!" The dealers pumped their fists and hollered their approval. The guide knew how to charm these guys and anticipated a big tip at the end of the day. He asked for a volunteer to take the last position in line and make sure no one fell behind. Jack quickly raised his hand. Everyone got in the dune buggies. The guide took his position in the vehicle at the front of the line and called out "Sand and sun, here we come!" They were off.

The dune buggies bounced and swerved as the dealers were getting the hang of controlling them. One driver veered off the side of the trail and a plume of sand and dirt shot into the air. The others laughed and called him a pussy. Cheryl shook her head. *It's going to be a long afternoon with these macho jerks.*

Drinking and bragging continued as they bounced through the desert. After an hour, the guide called a rest stop next to a stand of majestic saguaro cactus, some over thirty feet tall. He described the magnificence of these plants, which are adapted to the harsh desert conditions and can survive months without rain. While he spoke, one of the drunken dealers wandered behind him and began to carve his initials into a saguaro. The guide ran to stop him—it was a serious violation of state law to do anything that harms a saguaro—but he was shouted down by the group, who rushed to stand between him and the carver. Jack pulled the agitated guide to one side. "Let it go. I'll take responsibility."

"I could lose my license if I don't report this. It's a felony!"

Jack slipped him a hundred dollar bill to forget the whole thing.

Soon they were off again. They entered a large canyon with glorious rock formations of red and pink. The trail was bumpy and the pace was fast. Jack let out a "Yee-hah!" as the dune buggy went airborne briefly. Before long, Cheryl felt sick to her stomach. She held onto the roll bar and breathed deeply, but it wasn't helping. She told Jack to stop so she could throw up. She walked behind a rock and heaved her guts out. She staggered back to the dune buggy and took a long drink from her water bottle. When she got into the vehicle, the others were no longer in sight. "No problem, we'll catch up!" Jack said as he sped off, following the tracks in the sand. Then the trail ended in an expanse of smooth exposed rock. Tracks led off in several directions. Jack couldn't tell which ones belonged to today's tour. He picked one and drove down it for a while. These tracks petered out in more rocks. He stopped and looked around, then drove back to the first area of rock. "We must have taken the wrong trail. They obviously went the other way."

More bumping as he took a different route. Cheryl didn't like this one bit. A sickening sense of foreboding rose inside her. Jack followed the second trail, which ended in a closed box canyon. He turned back and followed a third set of tracks. As he began to realize he was disoriented, he drove faster, making sudden turns. Cheryl squeezed the roll bar in front of her as tight as she could.

After yet another trail faded out, he said, "Oh now I know where to go." He backed up and took yet another fork. It too led nowhere. He got out his phone to call someone, but there was no signal. They were lost. Cheryl rocked back and forth and stared blankly. Her anxiety had overwhelmed her. Jack glanced at her and was worried. "The best thing for us to do is to wait here. They'll come back to find us before long. That's what the guide is paid to do. He wouldn't have this job if he went around losing customers. He either gets back here soon, or I'll make sure he's fired by sunset."

Cheryl gave him a withering look. "You're the one who got us lost!"

"Me? If you hadn't been tossing your cookies, we would still be with the group."

"Oh, it's my fault? If you hadn't been showing off and driving like a maniac, I wouldn't have barfed in the first place. Just because you think you're Mr. Big Shot Salesman doesn't mean you can blame everyone else when you screw up!"

For once, Jack was quiet and stared straight ahead. Cheryl was getting fired up. "Do you have any idea how many people at SDI warned me about you?"

He gave her a surprised look. Cheryl was done being polite and cautious with him. She knew she was crossing a line, but having this job to pay off her credit cards and keep her apartment wasn't worth dying out here in the desert.

"Yeah, they all hate you. God's anointed asshole." No one had ever said anything like this to Jack before.

"Screw 'em and screw you! None of you would have jobs if it weren't for me."

Jack got out of the dune buggy to stretch his legs. Cheryl watched him looking idly at a group of boulders. "Watch out for rattlesnakes!" she shouted.

"Where?"

"Right over there," she pointed. "One just went behind that rock."

He hopped back into the dune buggy and pulled his legs up.

"Gotcha!" she said with a laugh.

"Don't joke about snakes!"

She had found his weak spot. "How do you feel about scorpions and Gila monsters? At the hotel I read we need to watch out for them too." She delighted in poking at his fears.

The sun slowly moved lower in the west and its intensity began to dim. A cold gust of wind blew through the canyon. Winter days were short, even in Arizona. Both Cheryl and Jack were dressed lightly for the heat of the afternoon. When the sun dipped below the ridgeline above them, the falling temperature was inescapable. Cheryl was shocked at how quickly the desert heat disappeared after the sun set. Jack said to her "The combination of high altitude and low humidity means the atmosphere doesn't retain heat. I've seen the same thing elk hunting in Montana."

"Will you shut up!" she yelled, sick of his mansplaining. She got out of the dune buggy to look at the emergency kit strapped on the back. It was disappointing, with nothing more than matches, a foil space blanket, a few expired energy bars, water bottles, and the pint of tequila. She held up the matches, "I'm building a fire. No need to freeze our butts off." She walked around gathering sticks. Jack, whose fear of rattlesnakes was growing as the light faded, stayed put. She looked back at him. "Hey! Do I have to do this by myself?" Reluctantly, he got out of the dune buggy. When he saw a stick, he kicked at it to make sure no creatures were underneath before picking it up. She found his fear both annoying and amusing. Soon they had piled up enough fuel and Cheryl lit a fire. As the flames crackled, Jack told her not to worry. The hotel or the tour company would come for them.

"No they won't!" Cheryl said. "You got us lost and we're going to be stuck out here all night."

"Let's make it interesting. I'll bet you fifty bucks someone is here soon. Probably in the next hour."

"Does everything have to be about money?"

"Alright, alright. A token bet. Five bucks. You can't complain about that."

They stared at their little fire. She despised him and he was irritated by her. A loud *Whooo* startled them. "What the hell was that?" Jack said.

"An owl, I think."

"Jesus! What the hell else is out here?" He looked around warily. Cheryl threw a few more sticks onto the fire. When the flames rose up, she spotted the silhouette of the owl at the top of a scrub tree about twenty feet away. She pointed it out to Jack. He said, "Jesus, it's huge!"

Cheryl poked at the fire and the sparks flared up. They were reflected in the owl's large eyes. "He's watching us," she said, delighting in Jack's discomfort. She took a drink from her water bottle. He pointed at it and asked, "What does C4 stand for?"

"Climate Crisis Coordinating Committee. I volunteer with them."

"What do they do?"

"Only the most important work in the world. We fight climate change."

"Why is that such a big deal? As far as I can see, all global warming means, if it's even real, is don't go to Arizona in the summer and don't buy beachfront property in Florida. I can live with a few inconveniences. Why get all upset about it?"

Cheryl rolled her eyes. "You're happy to let the world fall apart—floods, droughts, starvation, and much more— just so you can hang on to your money and pathetic comforts. It's disgusting."

Jack was unruffled. Objections from customers energized him. They were opportunities, problems to solve. "Okay, so how's the noble fight going?"

"Not so great. The world is full of stupid, greedy people who don't want to face reality." She gave him a pointed stare to show him exactly who she was talking about.

"Hell, I knew that a long time ago. Every salesman worth his salt knows it too. Your problem is nobody's buying what you're selling."

"We're not selling anything, we're educating!"

"I'll let you in on a little secret, Ricard. It's all selling. What I do and what you want to do. Nothing happens unless someone is out there selling. That's how the world works.

"The only reason you sell is to make a buck. You don't give a damn about anything but your bank account. You're more than happy to help Mega Motors wreck the environment, as long as you can get rich along the way. The greed of people like you is going to get us all killed!"

Cheryl immediately regretted saying that. Once again, she had gone too far in her righteous indignation, just like at the plumbing company. Would this little outburst get her fired too?

But Jack laughed. "You're probably right. Mega may be bad, but they pay my salary, your salary, and a lot more. You could even the score by donating the money you make to your climate committee."

"I need that money!"

"And I need mine. None of us are pure. So let's not waste time trying to fool ourselves. The thing is, I know how to play the game and the vast majority of other people, including you, my dear, don't. Am I supposed to make sacrifices to take care of them? I don't think so."

"You've sold your soul to a heartless corporation."

"Let me tell you the actual truth about these 'heartless corporations.' Most of the people who work at them are just regular schmucks, who want to gather enough acorns to make it through the winter. They're no better or worse than anybody else. Take Vince Maranga, for example. He has two smart, beautiful daughters who want to go to fancy colleges. Making sure they can do that—by paying for it—is the only thing he cares about. He'll tie himself in all kinds of knots, like we saw yesterday, because he wants to see their smiling faces when they hold their diplomas. He doesn't spend two seconds worrying about the fate of Mega Motors, as long as it keeps contributing to his 529 plan. Walter Lydecker, the CEO, on the other hand, is a different animal. Your word 'heartless' fits him to a T. He'd sell out his mother if it would raise Mega's stock price."

"Are you any better? You'd sell out *your* mother to close a deal. You make no effort to hide it. That's why no one likes you."

"My clients love me."

She laughed. "You're nice to *them* because you want their money. Everyone else thinks you're a know-it-all blowhard."

"What do all your high-minded principles do for you? You have a shit job and are probably broke. Hope you're not offended when I say that, but I bet it's true."

"Screw you, Jack."

They sat quietly. Jack poked at the fire. They were both too irritated to talk and, at the same time, each knew that the other had made some good points. The sky had darkened, the first stars twinkled, and it kept getting colder.

"Do you believe in anything beyond yourself?" she asked.

He thought for a moment. "To be totally honest with you—no I don't. All I want is to enjoy the ride and have some nice stuff along the way. That's good enough for me. What do you believe in?"

"I believe in doing the right thing. And that lots of other people want to do the right thing too, if they understand the truth about what's going on."

"Don't count on that working, Ricard. The simple fact is that nobody—at least almost nobody—does a damn thing just because it's right or good or whatever you want to call it."

"I refuse to believe that people are that selfish."

"Get used to it."

"So we're doomed? Should we just give up?"

"Maybe. At least until you learn how to sell your product."

She decided to try a different approach. "Have you heard of the Greenland ice sheet?"

"No. What about it?"

"It's only the most important place on earth. Two miles thick and it covers almost seven hundred thousand square miles. And it's melting, because people like you keep pumping out carbon dioxide without a care in the world. When it melts all the way, sea level will rise twenty feet. A lot of your favorite golf courses will be under water. It's simple chemistry. Try selling your way out of that one."

"You're asking me to worry about a hypothetical possibility way off in the future? If that's your best sales pitch, then you and your precious movement are more clueless than I thought."

Cheryl fumed. *What an asshole!* Though she wondered if maybe what he was saying might be kind of right.

It was so dark they couldn't see anything beyond the glow of the fire. Jack got up and retrieved the energy bars and space blanket from the emergency kit. He tossed an energy bar to Cheryl, then unfolded the blanket. "This is all we got, but it's big enough for both of us."

Cheryl insisted on sitting back-to-back while wrapped in the space blanket. She didn't want to look at him or feel his breath. They were running out of sticks for the fire, so Jack had to ration them to the point where it provided almost no warmth. He could feel Cheryl shivering behind him. He decided to distract her by talking—about his favorite subject.

"I know you think selling is evil, but it's what makes the world go round. When you meet with a client and do it right, it's like a beautiful song you can't stop humming. I've read a ton of books about how to sell. Classics like Ziglar and Carnegie, and the newer stuff. Mostly, they try to pump up the guys who don't really want to be salespeople and are kind of embarrassed by what they do. Which is just about everyone in the business. Only a few of us operate on a higher level. The books make selling sound like something altruistic. You're trying to solve the customer's problem and help them get what they really, really need. Blah, blah, blah. That's true as far as it goes, but it's a fig leaf. You want to make the customer *believe* that you're trying to solve his problem. There's a big difference. I once saw a comedian on the Tonight Show who said, 'When you can fake sincerity you've got it made.' He was joking, but was onto something. I know all about honesty. I listened to a podcast about it on the way to the golf course last week. Where, I'll have you know, I didn't mess with my lie one time in eighteen holes. I was tempted as hell, but I didn't give in."

"You went a whole day without cheating? I'm so impressed."

Jack ignored her sarcasm and continued. He was on a roll. "Everybody wants to buy, but no one wants to be sold. When you buy something, you're taking charge, making a decision. Doesn't that feel good? You bet it does. On the other hand, when you're being sold, you're a chump who is being manipulated by a salesperson. You're embarrassed and don't want to admit that to anyone, not even to yourself. So the job of the salesperson is to sell the customer while orchestrating everything so the customer sees himself as a bold visionary making a wise choice completely out of his free will. The skilled salesperson leaves no trace. He asks harmless questions and drops little hints, all to lead the customer down the path to grandma's house. You only want to be his helpful friend."

"Are your customers stupid enough to fall for that?"

"Playing the customer's emotions is the art. It has to be done differently for each person. You need to know what they want, what they fear, and what will touch their heartstrings. Whatever it takes to close a sale, without them realizing what you're up to. If your customer suspects you're trying to 'close' them, you've just lost. You need to know when to reveal, when to hold back, when to reassure, and when to create FUD. It's a talent that can't be taught."

"What is FUD?"

"F-U-D. Fear, uncertainty, and doubt. The great motivators of the universe. You'll never get anywhere with your climate change nonsense until you realize that. People buy emotionally. It's always been that way, ever since the first guy went cave to cave selling a better club for bashing sabretooth tigers. Every customer I've dealt with is terrified of making the wrong decision. Some are better at hiding it than others. Some even fool themselves with a heaping truckload of rationalizing bullshit. But at the moment of truth, when they have to decide whether to buy or not to buy, fear takes over. I sell to people who have big corporate jobs that come with tons of money, status, and ego stroking. They all know if they make the wrong decision, everything can be gone in a heartbeat. Even CEOs can get booted off the gravy train. That can put a real dent in your wallet, but the loss of status—suddenly becoming a nobody—is much worse. The more they crave the praise and the high life, the easier it is for me to steer them into what they need to do—buy what I'm selling."

"Don't *you* crave the high life? The resorts? The golf courses?"

"Good question, as the consultants like to say, but the answer is no. When I'm at home with the wife, I'm perfectly content to watch Netflix and eat microwaved dinners from Trader Joe's. All I want out of this game is to pile up enough cash so I can tell everyone to go screw themselves. If I can renew the Mega Motors account for one more cycle, I'll just about be there. Then it'll be Trader Joe's, golf, and G&Ts to my heart's content."

He waited for her to say something. He enjoyed having a rapt audience. But she was quiet, so he kept going.

"My job forces me to look into the soul of my customer. I don't recommend it for the faint-hearted. Why do you think I need my G&Ts? I see things about people that I'd rather not. But those are what make the quarters pour out of the slot machine into my little plastic bucket.

"The only other eternal principle I believe in is incompetence. Most customers make dumb decisions most of the time. Which is great because it gives me opportunities to rescue them from their own screw-ups. There's a scientific law, one of the tech nerds told me over a drink, called entropy. Which means that, left alone, everything goes to shit sooner or later. That's a comforting thought that helps me sleep at night."

Jack watched the throbbing red embers of the dying fire. "Are you ready for me to teach you about real selling, Ricard? If you could get down off your high horse, you might actually have some talent for it."

He listened but, instead of saying something, she let out a wheezy snore. She had fallen asleep while he was spouting off. He tossed the last sticks on the fire and looked up at the countless stars in the clear sky above. He got the bottle of tequila out of the cooler and took a swig. He hoped that no rattlesnake would try to crawl under the blanket to get warm.

Jack felt a tap on his shoulder. He startled awake and raised his hand to block the flashlight shining in his face. "Are you from Off-Road Arizona? Thank God!"

"No, I'm not and God has nothing to do with it."

"Then you must be from the hotel."

"Nope. They won't come out here in the dark. Too dangerous."

Jack poked Cheryl in the ribs to wake her. She was a sound sleeper. "Hey, rise and shine Ricard. You owe me five bucks."

The visitor was holding the reins of a horse. He wore a long black coat and an oversize cowboy hat. "I saw your fire and came to find out what was going on. Do you have gas in your vehicle?"

"Yeah, but we're lost, so it made sense to stop and wait for morning."

"I'll take you where you can warm up, eat, and rest. We can be there in a half hour."

"Do you have a phone that works? Mine can't get a signal. I'm in charge of a really important event back in Scottsdale and I need to get in touch with my team ASAP. It's urgent!"

"Follow me." The man climbed onto his horse.

Cheryl was just waking up and still groggy. She had never been this cold in her life. Her feet were numb and felt like blocks of wood when she stood up. *Who is this guy with a cowboy hat and horse? Where is he taking us?* Jack stomped out the embers of the fire and got in the dune buggy. He gestured impatiently for her to join him. She had a weird feeling about this, but Jack was eager to go and she couldn't think of much that would be worse than spending the whole miserable night outside, so she didn't object.

Jack started the dune buggy's engine and its loud roar shook her out of her stupor. The horseman led them into a narrow canyon. The dune buggy's headlights bounced with every rock as Jack carefully followed him. It was slow going. Cheryl shivered and pulled the foil blanket tightly around her as they bumped along a dry creek bed. A pincushion of stars above was framed by black silhouettes of rock walls on either side. They wound through the canyon, then reached a flat plateau, where the full expanse of the night sky opened above them. A few minutes later, they came to a slightly wider canyon.

The horseman halted and waited for the dune buggy to catch up. He pointed to a narrow path between two tall rock outcroppings and gestured for them to follow. There were only a few inches of clearance on either side of the dune buggy so Jack drove extra slowly. Cheryl saw a faint luminescence up ahead. The horseman signaled that he was turning left. They rounded a steep, almost vertical, wall of rock. A dazzling sight revealed itself. Three glowing shapes were covered with intricate, multicolored, geometric patterns. A cube and a pyramid, each about twenty feet tall, flanked the largest structure, a tapered cylinder topped with a dome. Low, horizontal shapes connected the three. The horseman signaled to Jack to park the dune buggy in front of the cylinder. He then dismounted and tied the reins of his horse to a hitching post. When Jack turned off the dune buggy's headlights, the glowing buildings provided the only light. They reminded Cheryl of the plastic blocks she loved playing with when she was a child—colored squares and triangles with magnetic edges which could be assembled into any shape imaginable.

"Where the hell are we?" Jack asked.

"Welcome to Vastiati," the horseman said, "I apologize for my rudeness, my name is Tycho." He reached out to shake hands.

"Jack Weatherly," Jack said.

"Please, first name only, Jack. We're all friends here."

Cheryl took the cue and gave only her first name as she shook Tycho's hand.

"Let's get you inside," Tycho said. They walked to the cylinder. He touched the wall and a door slid open. They entered a high-ceilinged room. The interior surfaces glowed with the same pattern as the outside. Artwork adorned the walls, except for one which was lined with tall bookshelves. About a dozen people were sitting around a long wooden table. Some reading, others drawing, and a few playing chess. Most were wearing outdoor clothes, like fleece and flannel shirts. One woman was dressed in black with glittering sequins. Cheryl basked in the warmth as she took in this sight.

"Friends, welcome Cheryl and Jack, who were lost," Tycho said.

"But now you're found." The sequined woman stood up and smiled. "We're honored to be of assistance. I'm Vera."

"Are you in charge here?" asked Jack.

"No one's in charge."

"Can you take us to the highway?"

"It's too dangerous in the dark."

"Your pal Tycho brought us here in the dark."

"You were in trouble. Now you're safe until morning"

"You don't understand. I'm responsible for a meeting of a thousand people that's going on in Scottsdale right now. I need to get back there as soon as possible."

Vera smiled. Jack wanted to show Cheryl that he could get his way. "I can pay you to take us to the highway." He got out his wallet and held up a credit card. "I also have cash, not that much, two hundred bucks."

"Money isn't the answer here."

"You drive a hard bargain. Okay. Five hundred bucks—two hundred now, the rest when I find an ATM."

Vera laughed. "Tycho will lead you to the highway in the morning, free of charge. Until then, you're our guests."

Cheryl noticed that all the people in the room were staring at Jack. A few whispered to each other. She was embarrassed by his arrogance.

"This is very important! Can I at least contact my team?"

"I'm afraid we have no phone or internet."

Jack scowled and crossed his arms to show his displeasure.

"You will be in Scottsdale tomorrow and all will be well. Our entire lives are but a blink in the majesty of time. Accept your visit here as a gift from the universe."

Someone brought food for Jack and Cheryl. As she ate her hot soup—beans, mushrooms, and spinach in a rich brown broth—she enjoyed Jack's frustration that he couldn't get his way. *Serves him right. The world doesn't revolve around his stupid dealer meeting.* She was finally getting warm. Her toes tingled as they thawed out. One of the people brought coats for her and Jack. They were polite, then went back to their reading and whispered conversations. Everyone seemed nice enough, but they were distant.

Jack slurped his soup. His heel bounced up and down with nervous energy. "Between that moron Vince and that prima donna Meadows, the whole meeting could be going to hell while I'm stuck here twiddling my thumbs." He nodded his head towards the others in the room. "How do they live like this? We're off the goddamned grid!"

"Some people don't want electronics running their lives all the time."

"It's barbaric!" He leaned close to her and whispered, "I think this place is some kind of cult. They look brainwashed. Bunch of wackos."

She hissed at him to be quiet. She had been savoring the soup, but now she glanced around warily. She wondered if there was a reason to be frightened or if he was just being paranoid. Jack sulked. He didn't like being brushed off. He was used to people being impressed by his aura of success.

"Look at the bright side," Cheryl said with a smile. "Tycho saved you from the rattlesnakes."

Vera sat down next to them. Jack decided he would make small talk to see if he could get a better handle on who these people were. "Where do you get your power if this place is off the grid?"

"We use a fusion reactor."

"You're kidding me!"

"No. It's very reliable."

"Can we see it?"

"Not now. In the morning."

"Is it safe?"

"Oh yes, very safe. It's ninety-three million miles away." Everyone in the room giggled. So did Cheryl. Jack was confused. She poked him. "It's the sun, dummy."

Vera poured mugs of tea for Cheryl and Jack. Cheryl asked her, "What do you do here?"

"At Vastiati, we try to learn as much as we can."

"About what?"

"Science, the stars and, above all, ourselves. We believe that study and learning is the most important work that anyone can do. What about you, Cheryl? What do you study?"

The question came out of left field, so Cheryl had to think for a moment before answering. "How to slow climate change and save the planet. What will make the most difference. And why it's so hard to convince people to do anything about it."

"Ahh. Excellent! Like us, you study science and big, important questions. What have you learned?"

"The solutions are right in front of us, but people are selfish and don't want to change. So it keeps getting worse."

"And you, Jack? What do you study?"

"I make things happen by selling—getting people to make decisions."

"You must have to study a lot to do that."

"I guess I study human nature. That's the key to selling."

"How wonderful! People are the most fascinating. What have you learned?"

He had to think for a moment. "People want to be fooled. All you have to do is tell them what they want to hear. It's not that hard." Cheryl was appalled by his cynicism, though she wasn't surprised.

"We have learned the exact same thing!" Vera said with pleasure. "It takes a lot of work to avoid delusion. We are fooled when we see what we want to see. It's a trick of the mind. 'Rose colored glasses' as the old saying goes. Also, we are fooled when we believe that something outside of us will make us happy or that we can control other people. Don't you agree?"

"Most people have no real idea about what's good for them. I guide them to an answer."

Vera nodded. "I can see why you and Cheryl are friends. You make a perfect team. She studies what needs to be done and you study people—the ones who have to do it." Cheryl resented the idea of being lumped in with Jack.

Vera stood up and collected the soup bowls. "Tonight is a special night. There is no moon, so we can see the universe with clarity. A profound experience. We'll begin shortly. Until then, please feel free to look at our library."

Cheryl and Jack walked over to the bookshelves. Most of the books were about science—astronomy, physics, biology, both textbooks and biographies of people like Newton, Darwin, and Einstein. Cheryl whispered to Jack, "I hope you realize that what you were saying was a big load of crap."

"Vera didn't think so."

"So she's the expert now? Because she agreed with you?" Cheryl snorted sarcastically. "When we got here, you thought this place was a cult."

"I still don't like the way they stare at us. It's creepy as hell."

Just then, a chime sounded. A single note reverberated through the room. People stopped whatever they were doing and returned to sit around the table. Vera gestured for Cheryl and Jack to take seats. She and Tycho stood at the head of the table. Tycho spoke.

"We will prepare ourselves to journey into the vast universe."

The lights in the room dimmed, then went out entirely.

"Our eyes need time to adjust before we can clearly witness the night sky. It will take several minutes."

They all sat in darkness. At first, Cheryl and Jack couldn't see a thing. It was like being in a cave. Cheryl waved her hand in front of her face. Nothing.

Vera began to speak, softly and hypnotically.

"Tonight, we gaze outward to the stars and open our eyes to their beauty."

The others in the room responded in unison. "All the beauty."

"We gaze inward to our tiny planet and open our eyes to the interconnected life forms that it nurtures."

"All the life."

"We give thanks to the experiences that teach us. To suffering."

"All the suffering."

"To joy."

"All the joy."

"To losses."

"All the losses."

"To triumphs."

"All the triumphs."

"To fear."

"All the fear."

"To love."

"All the love."

"For our guest Cheryl, we gaze outward with hope for our beautiful planet."

"All the hope."

"We gaze inward to the work we must do."

"All the work."

"And for our guest Jack, we gaze outward to infinite possibilities."

"All the possibilities."

"We gaze inward to find the best words."

"All the words."

"We remember this truth: everything we can imagine is happening at this very moment. Right now, some are born and others die. For some, today is the best day of their life and for others, the worst day. All are equal as we huddle together on our tiny speck of dust in the vastness. The stars shine no matter what we do. On our little speck we can only hurt ourselves, or help ourselves, and the little ones."

"All the little ones."

Cheryl felt the deep calm of Vera's chant and the soft voices all around her. Jack was getting nervous again. It sounded like cult talk to him.

A dim red light came on, a flashlight in Tycho's hand. He opened the door and the group filed outside. The glow on the buildings had been turned off, so the only light came from his red flashlight, which pointed the way. Cheryl and Jack looked upward. Their eyes had acclimated to the dark and now they were overwhelmed by the canopy of stars and the pale ribbon of the Milky Way. "Before we go further," Vera said, "Stand here a short while and take in the beauty spread out above us—our home."

After a moment of silence, Tycho pointed out the path of white flagstones, barely visible beneath their feet, to Cheryl and Jack. "This path represents our galaxy, the Milky Way, with its spiral arms and large central disk. A few hundred billion stars spread across almost ninety thousand light years." As they walked across the disk, he pointed to the ribbon above. "The central disk alone is home to billions of stars. From here on earth, we can see a side view of that disk above us." The group continued along a narrowing arm of the path. They arrived at a telescope, which was about seven feet tall, mounted on a pedestal near the end of the spiral path. "This place on the path mirrors the location of our solar system in the Milky Way."

"We plant our feet on the ground and gaze to the heavens again, children," Vera said. "As above, so below." The group repeated her words, "As above, so below." Jack leaned over to Cheryl and whispered, "I don't have time for these wackadoodles." She elbowed him in the ribs. "Shut up! They can hear you."

The group formed a circle around the pedestal so each one could take a turn looking through the telescope. Tycho explained the first object of the night's viewing. "We'll begin our voyage in our own neighborhood, the solar system, to observe the most striking of all planets—Saturn with its graceful wreath of rings."

Vera led Cheryl and Jack to the pedestal. "As our guests, please go first." Cheryl stepped onto a small platform next to the telescope and Tycho guided her to the rubber eyepiece. The pale yellow sphere of Saturn and its slanted disk of rings filled her view. "The rings are made of countless pieces of ice, from the microscopic to the size of boulders, that orbit the planet. What sculpts them into these perfect rings? The force that brings all of us together—gravity. Every object attracts every other object. Given enough time, this simple force created the exquisite delicacy of Saturn's rings."

When Cheryl finished looking, Vera said, "On and on." The group responded, "And on." Then it was Jack's turn. He looked for just a few seconds. Saturn didn't look like much to him. He had seen plenty of pictures of it. When he finished, Vera said again, "On and on," followed by the group "And on."

After each person finished their turn at the telescope, they said "On and on" as they stepped down from the platform, with the group echoing "and on." Tycho aimed the telescope at the second object. "We look at these stars every time we come out here. They're one of the galaxy's greatest hits—the gorgeous Pleiades, also called the Seven Sisters."

Again, Cheryl went first. She saw a cluster of bluish stars in the eyepiece. They were indeed gorgeous, like gems against the darkness. "The Pleiades are also our neighbors, out here at our end of the Milky Way. A mere 444 light years from earth."

"Is that close?" Cheryl asked.

"Compared to what? The light we saw from Saturn traveled to our telescope in about eighty-three minutes. This light from the Pleiades took 444 *years* to get here. If you want to know how far that is in miles, we'll be running out of zeroes." This time, when Cheryl stepped down she said "On and on" herself. The group responded.

Next, Jack took a brief turn at the telescope. These stars looked nice enough, but as far as he was concerned, all stars were pretty much the same. He was getting tired of this game and hoped Vera and Tycho would have a comfortable bed for him. When he stepped down off the platform, he purposely didn't say "On and on." Vera said it for him.

There was considerable oohing and ahhing as the others in the group took their turns looking at the Pleiades. Then Vera said they would look at one more object tonight. As Tycho aimed the telescope, she said "Jack, this is a good one for you. Please go first."

Jack stepped onto the platform and peered through the eyepiece. "It's fuzzy. Out of focus." Tycho looked to check. "The focus is sharp. That's what we wanted you to see."

Jack looked again. Tycho continued, "It appears to be fuzzy because it's not a star. It's a galaxy with about a trillion stars. This galaxy, the Pinwheel Galaxy or M101, is twenty-one million light years away, far beyond our own Milky Way. With very powerful telescopes, much stronger than this one, galaxies can be seen at almost every spot in the sky, even in places that look empty through this scope." Jack kept looking. He had never thought about anything like this.

Vera moved close to Jack. "Consider the billions of worlds within that little piece of fuzz. The countless lives of beings who are unimaginable to us."

Jack couldn't take his eye off the eyepiece.

"Everything is in there, Jack, and we'll never know. All we see is the little smudge. And we look the same to them."

"What about space travel? Couldn't we go there someday?"

"We could never live long enough to reach the Pinwheel Galaxy. The human species won't live long enough to get there."

"What about wormholes or hyperspace jumps?"

"It doesn't work like in the movies. We can look, but we can't touch. We can imagine, like we're doing now. But we're still stuck here and they're stuck there."

"That's depressing."

"Is it? Every one of us is just a smudge to someone out there. That's the truth of the universe. We can do whatever we choose, as long as we do it here. The question is what should we choose?"

Jack fought against the thought of his insignificance. But looking at the smudge of billions of worlds was very confusing. There had to be an angle here somewhere. What would the guys who wrote the books on selling, like Zig Ziglar or Dale Carnegie, say? *Think of all the opportunities!* But there weren't any out in that smudge. This time, Jack said "On and on" when his turn was over.

When she looked, Cheryl felt very small—but also very light. The weight of the warming planet and human stupidity lifted off her shoulders. None of it mattered to the Pinwheel Galaxy. She felt free. But freedom brought a chill of fear and her mind raced. *Why would you do anything if you knew it made no difference whatsoever? What is fear in the face of whatsoever? What is courage?* These questions raced through Cheryl as she pressed against the rubber eyepiece of the telescope and photons from a trillion thermonuclear fireballs streamed across millions of years into the willing wonder of her eyes. They arrived so softly and silently and asked nothing of her. No voice of *should*. No *you must*. Her rage against greedy polluters and selfish idiots felt hollow. Beside the point. Though she didn't know what the point was. Light floated in through her cornea and the fluid of her eyeball to the photoreceptors of her retina. Then along the slender thread of her optic nerve into the unfathomable universe of her brain. She had seen stars before, but not like this.

The next morning, the group assembled outside the buildings. Vera said goodbye to Cheryl and Jack. "Thank you for coming to see us. I hope we were good hosts. I enjoyed our conversations. Keep studying—whatever you want. Serious study of any subject that fascinates you will lead you to deeper understanding of the beautiful and vast universe. Every piece of knowledge we learn generates more new questions and moments of wonder. A never-ending chain reaction. On and on."

"And on." A chorus of the people responded to Vera. Cheryl and Jack hadn't realized they were all listening.

Vera hugged Cheryl tightly. While in the embrace, she whispered into Cheryl's ear, then pulled back, looked her straight in the eye and nodded to emphasize her message. Then she hugged Jack the same way, whispering and then nodding for emphasis.

"Let's get you to the road so you can return to Scottsdale," Tycho said. He mounted his horse and pointed out the path. Vera and the others waved goodbye. Cheryl waved back to them as Jack drove the dune buggy away. They followed Tycho as he wound through canyon after canyon. Everything looked different in the daylight. The dune buggy bounced on the rocky trail. Jack concentrated on driving and Cheryl was lost in memories of the night before and Vera's whispered message. Eventually, they came to a blacktop county road. Tycho dismounted and pointed them in the direction of a gas station a few miles away. "I hope our paths cross again someday," he said as they all shook hands.

They watched Tycho ride his horse behind a hill and out of sight. Jack gunned the dune buggy and they sped away on the smooth pavement.

Common Sense

When they reached the gas station, Jack found a signal and called Vince, whose first words were "Where the hell have you been, Weatherly? We've had a helicopter out searching for you since dawn." Jack gave him the county route number and name on the sign above the gas station, *Acme Gas N Go*, so the helicopter could pick them up, then asked how the meeting was going. "While you were out on your little adventure, we had a string of near disasters. I had to step in to take care of them."

Whatever was happening, that idiot probably made it worse, Jack thought, as he gave Vince a soothing apology. Cheryl sent a text to Mary Ann to say they were okay. She was in the middle of directing the new model reveal and replied quickly with a heart emoji.

A throbbing beat in the sky turned into a deafening roar as the helicopter descended to land next to the gas station. The noise was almost unbearable for Cheryl after the tranquility of the night before. The rotor wash threw up a dust storm that stung her eyes. The tour guide hopped out and gave Jack and Cheryl hugs. He was both relieved that they were safe and mortified that he lost them the day before. He motioned them to the helicopter. Cheryl had never been in one before and hated rollercoasters and anything high and precarious. She was on the verge of a panic attack as she climbed in. The pilot saw her distress, handed her ear protection headphones, and helped her with her seatbelt. She squeezed the armrests tight as the helicopter took off. She relaxed a bit as she watched the desert passing by below. Jack and the tour guide were shouting into each other's ears as they flew. Jack waved his arms and pointed to the desert. The tour guide looked confused and shook his head. Jack looked angry. He gestured emphatically to the desert again. The tour guide shrugged and said something. From watching his mouth, Cheryl thought it might be "There's nothing out there." Jack's disgusted reply looked like "Yes there is, goddammit!"

The flight back to the hotel took less than fifteen minutes. Birds perching around the fountain on the front lawn scattered as the helicopter landed. Cheryl removed the headphones and heard Jack's last words to the tour guide, "I expect to see that full refund by next week!"

Jack and Cheryl ducked their heads to avoid the rotor wash as the helicopter quickly lifted into the blue sky above them. As they walked to the hotel entrance, Jack was seething with rage. "Guess what that motherfucker said to me. That he knows that desert country like the back of his hand and there are no buildings out there. Not a one! He thinks I was making the whole thing up, or dreaming. Did I make it up, Ricard?"

"No. I was there too. Totally real."

Jack stopped right after they entered the lobby. He took a deep breath and said to Cheryl, "Let's keep quiet about what happened last night. Just say we were stuck in the desert and it was cold as hell."

"Why?"

"I don't want more questions or funny looks from anybody. We don't need that. And it's none of their damn business anyway."

Cheryl nodded a half-hearted agreement.

"I mean it!" Jack emphasized.

"Okay! I heard you the first time."

Jack couldn't stand the idea of anyone doubting him like the tour guide did. He worked hard to be the guy whose words always counted, who everyone paid attention to.

They walked into the hotel ballroom wearing the dusty clothes from their desert ordeal. People were milling about during the break before the final event of the dealer meeting, the closing speech by the Mega Motors CEO. Mary Ann and the SDI technicians at the soundboard spotted them and rushed over. Amid hugs and pats on the back, Jack and Cheryl described their freezing night eating energy bars under the stars. They eagerly accepted the hot coffee and muffins that were handed to them. They didn't mention Vastiati.

Jack peppered Mary Ann with questions about everything he had missed. Soon, Vince appeared and clapped Jack on the back to welcome him, then listed all the screw-ups he had been forced to deal with. Jack listened with an impassive expression, though Cheryl could tell he was pissed as hell.

A wave of anxiety swept over Cheryl as she sipped her coffee. She desperately needed to be alone. She looked around the ballroom and spotted a stack of black equipment trunks in a far corner near the stage. No one paid any attention to her as she made her way over to it. She found a small space behind the trunks, just big enough for her to sit down in, with her back against the wall and her knees pulled up to her chest. She stared at a trunk in front of her that had *Property of SDI* stenciled on it in white and breathed slowly to try and calm down. Twenty-four hours of nonstop stimulation had caught up with her. She had never experienced anything like it—the drunken dealers, the bouncing dune buggy, vomiting, getting lost, the cold, the owl, Jack's nutty rant about selling, the loud, terrifying helicopter. After a few minutes, the hamster wheel of her mind began to slow and other images came to the fore—glowing buildings, the bowl of soup, chanting in the darkness, *All the beauty,* the telescope, the smudge of a trillion stars, Vera's parting whisper. As Cheryl practiced her slow breathing, these images helped her anxiety glide into curiosity. *What was all that about?*

The lights in the ballroom turned off and on to signal that the program was about to resume. Cheryl stood up and joined a thousand people returning to their seats. She found an empty one next to the sound board, in the row behind Jack and Vince.

The room darkened and the Mega Motors theme music began. In time with key beats in the music, spotlights highlighted the new model vehicles on the stage. The crowd cheered as each one was lit up. Lance Meadows walked to center stage, with his white hair gleaming in the spotlight. He gestured to the vehicles behind him. "I have a big problem, friends. I love every one of these incredible new Mega models, but even I don't have enough room at my Beverly Hills house for all of them. When I get home, I'm telling my wife one thing: We're gonna need a bigger garage!"

The dealers gave him a standing ovation. The influencers roamed the stage with their phones held high, careful not to get in front of Meadows.

"But, seriously, friends. It's been so wonderful to be here this week with all of you, the Mega Motors family. Memories I will always cherish. Now, I have the distinct pleasure to introduce the man of the hour, the chief executive officer of Mega Motors, our leader Walter Lydecker!"

Lydecker strode out to the center of the stage, waving to the audience. He shook hands with Meadows, then stood behind a podium. His name and face loomed large on the screen behind him. The applause went on until he signaled for quiet.

"When I look out at all of you here today and at the terrific new model vehicles behind me, I see one thing—an American success story. Together, we have built a business, and a community, that is unmatched in the history of the automobile industry. It's really something special. No, that's not quite right. The truth is *you* are something special—the best of America."

More applause and cheers.

"What I love most about this country is its common sense. As we learned in school, a pamphlet with that title inspired its founding. Common sense set this nation on its path to greatness. And common sense built the best economy the world has ever known.

"I see common sense whenever I spend time on the factory floor with the workers who assemble our Mega vehicles. You can't build a quality automobile and solve the countless problems that come up in the manufacturing process without a healthy dose of common sense. Every one of our skilled and dedicated employees knows that.

"And when I visit your dealerships, I see common sense in your showrooms, where your sales teams take time to understand each customer's transportation needs, then match them with the right Mega vehicle to meet those needs—for safety, style, performance, and efficiency. Common sense solutions that make their lives better. I see common sense in your service and parts departments, where your dedicated professionals help customers maintain the value of their automotive investments and enjoy the peace of mind that only safe, reliable transportation can bring them in this chaotic world. So we at Mega and you in the Mega dealerships are partners in common sense. A band of brothers and sisters with a commitment to the people who count the most—our customers. So let us always keep our focus on common sense. It will never let us down.

"Sadly, there are powerful forces today who don't share our belief. People who have never built a car want to dictate what kinds of vehicles we can build. People who have never sold or repaired a car want to tell you what kinds of vehicles you can sell to your customers and how you should maintain those vehicles. These people, the bureaucrats deep in the bowels of government and the busybodies of so-called 'environmental' organizations, think they know more about what our customers need than we do. I want to say one thing loud and clear about what they want to do to us and to you. It's not common sense!

"Even as we meet here today, they are writing rules about fuel efficiency and even about what power trains we can sell. These rules will increase costs for our customers, make their families less safe, and, by the way, drive many of you out of business. We won't allow this to happen! The path will be hard, but we will never give up. I promise you that Mega will keep talking common sense to the bureaucrats and busybodies. I ask you to join us in this crusade to allow our customers to buy the vehicles they want to buy. Because our customers also have common sense. They know how they want to spend their hard-earned money and what will bring them the confidence of safe, reliable transportation. If that transportation comes with good, old-fashioned American values—like style and flair, like the deep-throated rumble that says power, and like the smooth acceleration of a well-made driving machine—well, that's just common sense!"

The dealers interrupted him with loud cheers. Cheryl looked around and saw the rapt expressions of joy on their faces. Lydecker paused, then signaled for quiet.

"I have traveled the length and breadth of this great land, and I sense that the tide is turning. Many are beginning to wake up from the seductive fantasies peddled by the busybodies and nervous nellies. A change is coming and coming soon!

"I pledge to you that Mega Motors will keep fighting for common sense transportation policies. And I know that you, our most important partners, will join us to proudly hold the banner of common sense high. Together we will prevail and our customers will thank us for our sacred work.

"To common sense!"

Lydecker raised a clenched fist into the air. Cheers erupted as a thousand dealers leapt to their feet and applauded. Their chant echoed through the hotel ballroom, "Common sense! Common sense! Common sense!"

Hotel staff members appeared in the aisles handing out lapel buttons that read "Common Sense."

Cheryl was infuriated. *He called the people who are trying to save the planet for everyone's children "busybodies!" He's talking about me, C4, even Annabelle!* She watched the dealers high-fiving each other as they began to file out of the ballroom. Jack was smiling and shaking hands with Vince, Mary Ann, and the technicians. He came over to Cheryl, "We pulled it off, Ricard!" She looked at him blankly. He slapped her on the back and moved on to the next person. She felt slimy and soiled for having gotten herself into this awful place.

Within two hours, the hotel emptied out as a thousand people jostled for buses, taxis, and Ubers to the airport. Jack headed to a meeting with a different client halfway across the country. Mary Ann, who had been the first to arrive in Scottsdale a week earlier, left for home. Cheryl's job was to oversee the production crews as they dismantled the stage and Mega Motors signage and packed up equipment for shipment back to SDI. If all went well, she would be able to wrap everything up and fly home on the redeye late that night. She was working on her laptop in the main ballroom when a technician came to her. "Everything is ready for the trucks. Sign this receipt and we'll start loading. Oh, we found this behind the stage. Don't know who it belongs to." He held up an expensive Louis Vuitton briefcase with no ID tag or embossed initials. Cheryl accepted it reluctantly. One more hassle to deal with.

All the Mega Motors people were already gone, so she checked with the security guards and the hotel's front desk. No one had reported a lost item. The unmarked briefcase was locked, so she couldn't look for anything that might identify its owner. She took it to her hotel room, then flopped onto the bed. She had been running on adrenaline for days and the accumulated fatigue hit her hard. She almost dozed off, then rallied. She had only a few hours before leaving for the airport and didn't want to miss her plane. She took a hot bath in her room's enormous tub. As she dried her hair, she remembered the briefcase on her bed. She knew she had to do something with it, but decided to pamper herself a little more first, while she still had the opportunity. She called room service and ordered the most expensive dish on the menu, a lobster dinner—even though lobster was on her list of environmentally destructive foods. After the harrowing, confusing, and wonderful night in the desert, and the creepiness of Lydecker's speech, she felt she deserved it. And she had learned how things were done at SDI—when expenses were going to be billed to the client, no one looked at them very hard.

Most likely, the briefcase belonged to one of the SDI or production company people, so Cheryl didn't want to leave it with the hotel; better to take it back to the office in St. Louis and deal with it there. To avoid a problem with airport security, she needed to know what was in it. Also, there might be something to identify the owner. From her true crime TV shows, she knew there were ways to get inside anything. After getting dressed, she searched on her laptop for YouTube videos about unlocking Louis Vuitton briefcases. A long list came up.

There was a knock on her door—the lobster dinner had arrived. She told the waiter to set the tray on the desk, then signed for it—adding an extra generous tip to the bill. *Spread the wealth! This guy needs it more than Mega does.* The meal was delicious—juicy lobster smothered in butter, sauteed asparagus, and baked potato with sour cream and chives. She hadn't eaten anything this tasty since …she couldn't remember when. As she ate, she checked emails and messages on her personal phone, which she hadn't looked at for two days. There were several texts from Amy, *How is it going out there? Having any fun?* as well a slew of emails from all the causes that never left her alone—mostly pleadings for donations by environmental organizations and political candidates who she had heard of only because they had somehow added her to their mailing lists. One email she was glad to see announced that Annabelle Sinkovsky's latest podcast episode had just dropped. Cheryl clicked to download it, so she could listen on the flight home.

She put her phone down and began looking through the YouTube videos on her laptop. One seemed promising. She ate a few more bites of her dinner, wiped her hands on the napkin, then followed the steps shown in the video. Unlocking the briefcase turned out to be remarkably easy, even on an expensive model. A paperclip and a safety pin were all it took. After a few minutes, the silver clasps popped open. The only thing inside was an accordion folder labeled *Project Common Sense — Confidential.* She took it out, then searched the briefcase's pockets, but didn't find anything else—no papers or business cards that might identify the owner.

The first document from the folder was a stapled memo, six pages long, entitled *Project Status,* dated just two days earlier. It described Project Common Sense as a "multimodal influence campaign to prevent ill-considered federal regulations and legislation that, if enacted, will have severe negative impacts on consumers, independent dealers, the automotive industry, and the broader U.S. economy." The list of regulations to be opposed included vehicle fuel efficiency standards, requirements for reduced tailpipe emissions, and subsidies for electric vehicles. The memo described the "successful efforts to enlist a wide range of organizations, media, and congressional staff to support the Project Common Sense initiative." The memo proposed a "coordinated rollout timetable" which focused on a date five weeks in the future, when participating organizations and individuals were to simultaneously announce their opposition to the proposed regulations. All had agreed to use terms like "rigorous technical review," "follow the science," "significant economic damage," and "vague, unsupported environmental benefits" in their communications. Announcements would be made independently, with no mention of Mega Motors as a party involved in the initiative. Attached to the memo was a set of talking points which had been provided to participating organizations for interviews and podcasts to be tailored to each organization's style. For example, "These well-meaning, but misguided, regulations would increase costs for American car buyers, while yielding only paltry benefits. A far better approach to the climate challenge will be to unleash the talents of automotive experts, without unnecessary restrictions and respect the common sense of consumers and motorists."

Cheryl read the memo with increasing horror. It referred to a spreadsheet which summarized expenses incurred to date and the recipients of "remuneration and other considerations." The last page of the memo requested approval to launch the final phase of the project in order to implement the rollout timetable. The word *OK* was written in blue ink, above a scrawled signature. It was mostly illegible, but Cheryl thought it could be Walter Lydecker's.

Next, she looked at the other documents in the folder, several multi-page spreadsheets. The first one listed many organizations, including some of the biggest environmental groups in the country. Columns had the amounts paid, dates, and comments. Most showed the budgeted amount paid within the last few months. Comments were "drove a hard bargain," "fully on board," "still reluctant," "need a new contact." A few said "refused, try again" or "refused, do not contact further," or "still in negotiation." Many six-figure payments were listed. Cheryl's eyes opened wide when she saw that the largest payment by far was for $5,000,000 to Annabelle Sinkovsky of the Climate Crisis Coordinating Committee. A scribbled comment in blue ink next to her name said "The big fish!" Cheryl stared at that one for a long time. *Annabelle? How could this possibly be true?*

Other spreadsheets listed payments to labor unions, journalists, and key congressional staff. Another summarized expenses for lobbyists and campaign contributions to candidates and PACs. It all added up to tens of millions of dollars.

Cheryl read the documents over and over. She had found something big, with the potential to upend the battle against climate change. The fact that Mega Motors was ready to bribe anyone and everyone to protect their profits was no surprise, but leaders in the environmental movement, especially Annabelle, taking the money was a shock. Cheryl was depressed at first, then angry. They had betrayed her and every other volunteer who marched, made phone calls, rang doorbells, and contributed money that they could barely afford. She was sure the local C4 groups didn't know anything about this. She kept looking at Annabelle's name on the spreadsheet. *She took five million bucks from these scumbags!* The rest of the lobster dinner, including the chocolate mousse dessert, remained uneaten.

Cheryl boarded a flight which left the Phoenix airport at midnight. The briefcase lay on the empty seat next to her. She wished she had never seen the damned thing and had no idea what to do about it. Her anxiety-filled mind raced at breakneck speed as possibilities bounced around. She could be a heroic whistleblower who revealed the lies and corruption of Mega Motors to a grateful public, with television interviews and her picture on front pages across the nation. That would be more attention than she could handle, and certainly get her canned from SDI. Did heroic whistleblowers get paid? Who could she tell her story to? Mega Motors had already bought off a long list of journalists. Also, would even the honest and uncorrupted ones believe a nobody like her?

Or, she could burn the papers, toss the briefcase in a dumpster, and pretend that nothing had happened. But she might still be found out. The technician would probably say, "Yeah, I found a briefcase then gave it to the lady from SDI." She could give the briefcase to Jack. Let Mr. Know-It-All decide what to do. He wouldn't be happy about this responsibility, which would complicate his mission of making money off Mega Motors. Would he grudgingly admire her honesty? She knew better than to count on that! And, after the way she had told him off out in the desert, she was sure he would fire her in a heartbeat, without a second thought.

Whatever she did, there was no going back to the way things were just a few hours ago, before the technician handed her the evil briefcase. How she wished she had a time machine, or a rocket to send it to the Pinwheel Galaxy. One way or another, she was now screwed.

The flight attendant woke Cheryl to tell her to prepare for landing and place the briefcase underneath the seat in front of her. She had dozed off without realizing it. As the plane descended in the dark, she watched the lights of the city below rising up to her. None of her possible next steps made any more sense now than they had before she fell asleep. She decided to do something that would keep her options open.

Cheryl got off the plane at five A.M., then stopped at her apartment to drop off her SDI laptop and phone, as well as her personal phone. She didn't want to take a chance on being tracked. She spotted the *People* magazine photo of Annabelle taped to the fridge. She tore it up and threw it in the trash, then put all the papers from the briefcase into a shopping bag and left her apartment. Her first stop was an ATM to get cash. Then she went to a twenty-four hour copy shop, where she was the only customer. After directing her to a copier, the attendant behind the counter went back to watching TikTok videos on his phone. She ran all the papers through the machine, making two copies of each page. She paid in cash, like in the true crime shows. She was worried the attendant might get nosy, but he was lost in the singsong voices and inane music of TikTok's airhead girls.

The morning sky was glowing orange as she drove home. She wiped down all the original pages of the documents (both sides), as well as the interior surfaces of the briefcase, to remove fingerprints (skipping this precaution was a frequent reason people got caught in the true crime shows), then placed the original papers back into the briefcase, hoping that they were in the right order, and locked it. She didn't want to leave any sign that it had been opened. She set the briefcase on the floor next to her door, then flopped into bed. She tossed and turned under the covers, as anxiety over her discovery pumped adrenaline through her body. It felt like she would never sleep again. But somehow she did, though not for long.

Time Bomb

The long corridor had a polished linoleum floor and gray metal lockers along both sides, as far as the eye could see. Cheryl's footsteps echoed as she walked alone. She was searching for something, but she couldn't remember what. A bell rang to signal the end of a class period. Doors opened between the banks of lockers and people poured out. They talked and laughed as they headed in different directions. Some jostled and bumped Cheryl as they pushed past. She recognized them as kids from her high school. The bell rang again and more students flooded into the corridor. Cheryl was trapped in the crowd. She couldn't move. She was terrified, suffocating. The bell rang a third time, louder than before. The deafening buzz morphed into a jangling ringtone. Her eyes fluttered open. The nightmare evaporated into nowhere. She reached for the phone on the nightstand. It was Jack.

"Do you know anything about a briefcase, Ricard?"

"Huh?"

"From the meeting. Maranga's messaged me ten times already this morning. He's going ballistic about a lost briefcase."

Cheryl glanced at the time. 7:55 AM. She stalled to clear her head. "You woke me up. I flew home on the redeye last night."

"Sorry. What about the briefcase?"

"One of the techs found a briefcase when they were packing up. Nothing had been reported lost to the hotel and all the Mega people were long gone. I brought it with me."

"Is it Maranga's?"

"How would I know? There's no tag or ID."

"What's in it?"

"No idea. It's locked." She was awake enough to know better than to tell Jack she'd opened it. He put her on hold for a minute. When he came back, he said "Vince wants you to hop on a plane to Detroit pronto and personally deliver it to him at Mega's headquarters."

"It's Saturday! I'm exhausted. Can I send it by courier?"

"No! He insists that you hand-carry it. He's terrified it could get lost again."

"Why is this such a big deal?"

"Damned if I know. He didn't say. Just go there, Ricard. I want to get him off my back. We have bigger fish to fry."

She sighed. "Okay."

"Mavis has you booked on the ten o'clock flight. Get moving."

Cheryl barely had time to dress, make a cup of coffee, and text Amy that she couldn't meet at the café—*Last minute work bullshit*—before driving to the airport.

She sat in the huge lobby of the Mega building in Detroit with the briefcase on her lap. Except for a security guard, it was empty on Saturday morning. An elevator door opened and Vince Maranga walked to her and held out his hand. She gave him the briefcase.

"You didn't open it, did you?"

"I wanted to so I could find out who to return it to. But it's locked." She did her best to look innocent. "I'll let Jack know you got it back safe and sound."

Vince said a quick thanks and turned back to the elevator. *I spend all day on airplanes and that's it? What a jerk!*

On the flight back to St. Louis, Cheryl was lost in a maze of questions and doomsday scenarios. She was sitting on a time bomb and the clock was ticking—one month to go before the announcement. She had to do something, but didn't know what. She alone had evidence of a giant conspiracy, involving people she had believed were on the side of good. She wished like hell that someone else could take this problem off her hands, someone who was smarter and braver than she. But it wasn't going anywhere. Why did this end up in her lap? How was quiet, shy, little Cheryl going to expose this massive crime against the planet? She should have given the briefcase to the hotel's Lost and Found and been done with it. But no, she tried to be responsible and now she was in a huge mess. She couldn't think of anybody she could hand this problem to. If the tour guide didn't believe Jack about the night in the desert, what hope did she have of convincing anyone of this much, much more far-fetched story? She wanted to run away and hide somewhere, anywhere. Being unemployed and broke was a lot easier than this. Life was simple then, back when Cheryl was nothing more than a self-sabotaging screw-up in a cruel world. She would happily trade this burden for that.

Cheryl got home late Saturday afternoon, too late for her weekly cleaning. After warming up leftovers for dinner, she fell asleep in front of the TV and didn't wake up for twelve hours. She cleaned the apartment furiously all day Sunday to try to regain some sense of order in her life. It felt weird to clean without the soundtrack of Annabelle's inspiring words. She wished Jeremy were there to play her something wonderful, even on her cheap speakers.

At work on Monday morning, Cheryl sat dazed in her cubicle. She did a little filing and made a few trivial phone calls. The dilemma of the briefcase discovery made it impossible to concentrate. Also, she figured she deserved a break after the craziness of Scottsdale and the emergency flight to Detroit. Paul emailed her to collect and organize all the vendor invoices from the dealer meeting, then begin assembling the master invoice from SDI to Mega Motors so it could be submitted before the end of the quarter, just a few days away. That was exactly what she needed—mindless work that was easy. As each invoice came in, both from vendors and from SDI departments, she entered it into a spreadsheet in a column next to the original budgeted item. She quickly noticed that with several vendors and departments, the invoiced amounts were a lot higher than the proposal budget. When she checked the invoices for supporting details to explain or justify the increases, she found little or nothing. $10,000 magically became $12,000 on one, while another added "logistics management" and "consumable supplies" to its long list of services provided with a new total amount $6,400 above the proposal. The vendors and departments didn't respond to her requests for clarification. She got a lot of automated out of office replies. She wrote an email to Paul, who was still out on paternity leave, to ask how he wanted her to handle the discrepancies. He replied, *Don't worry about them. Just enter the information into the spreadsheet, then Jack and I will review and approve the final invoice.* She remembered Jack's comment about burying the extra payments to Lance and the influencers. *So this is how it's done.*

To clear her head, Cheryl paid a midday visit to Final Sound. This time, Jeremy's T-shirt read *I'm Your Man*.

"Who's that for?" Cheryl asked, pointing to the shirt.

"For anyone who'll have me. I might get lucky someday."

Cheryl smiled. "Maybe you'll get lucky if you give me another dose of amazing music."

Jeremy made a theatrical bow. "Your wish is my command. Step into the listening chamber." As Cheryl settled into one of the leather sofas, he said. "Last time I played you an instrumental from India. Today, we'll do poetry."

"I want music!"

"This album is plenty musical, but written by a poet."

He returned to the control booth and dimmed the lights in the preview room. A stately waltz rhythm filled the air, followed by a plaintive electronic oboe melody, then the words "If you want a lover, I'll do anything you ask me to." Cheryl blushed and was glad he couldn't see her. A few lines later, she heard the chorus "Here I stand. I'm your man," which brought another smile to her face. The Final Sound speakers brought the singer's raspy voice only inches from Cheryl's ear, like every ounce of his passion and eloquence was meant just for her.

Jeremy came out when the album ended.

"Okay, tell me, who was that guy?" Cheryl asked.

He made another deep bow. "The one and only Leonard Cohen!"

"Jeremy, I have a question. Does it ever bother you what our clients do?"

"The shameless greed? The boorishness? Or the planet raping?"

"All of it."

He thought for a moment as he delicately coiled an audio cable into perfect circles. "I know the score. Sometimes, when I'm in the control room and clients are out here, they think no one can hear them. You wouldn't believe the nasty jokes, the cackling about insider deals and the suckers their companies are ripping off."

"I'd believe it. So what do you do?"

"Nothing. Once I had the bright idea to slip some subliminal messages into an audio track. Stuff like *We're liars. Don't buy our useless junk.* I'd read a book about using subliminal messages in advertising to trick people. So I did it and felt pretty good about myself. The piece went out and nobody noticed. Turns out that book about subliminal advertising was bullshit." He shrugged his shoulders. "I know I'm a whore, but I can live with that. If I quit this job, there are plenty of other whores waiting in line to take my place."

On Wednesday morning, Paul took a break from his paternity leave to come in and lead the team debrief of the Mega Motors dealer meeting. "What went well, what can we do better next time?" The discussion was mostly either mutual pats on the back ("The new model-reveal went off without a hitch and the lighting was spectacular.") or innocuous trivialities. ("The staging crew was completely professional. We should hire that company again.")

Mary Ann thanked Cheryl for her help with the "talent problem" at the rehearsal. Jack chimed in with "Ricard did a great job the whole time. And was a good sport when we were freezing our asses in the desert all night. She had to put up with me and my stories. I wouldn't wish that on anyone." That got a chuckle out of the team, who had heard all about Jack and Cheryl's ordeal—without, of course, its most surprising development. "Ricard also saved the day when Maranga got bent out of shape over a lost briefcase. He always finds something to be upset about."

At the end of the meeting, Jack said. "Lydecker wants to meet with me about something. I have an appointment for next week. Don't know if it's good or bad. We'll see."

Junk Food

Other than spending her days in the office, Cheryl hunkered down in her apartment all week. She couldn't face dealing with people, not even Amy. She tossed her healthy eating habits out the window and binged on junk food that she normally avoided—chips and ice cream. For years, the environmental movement had been her anchor, a cause that was undeniably good and important. Whatever else was going on in her life, she was proud to be a climate warrior.

Now she saw that the game was rigged. Her heroes were slimy sellouts, no better than the greedy corporations that were dragging the planet to hell. With her world turned upside down, she went through a repeating cycle of anger and depression. She was furious with both Annabelle and the original environmental asshole, her college boyfriend Todd, who had gotten her started on the climate change cause in the first place, only to dump her for greener pastures. (The pun brought the only smile she had the whole week.) She was depressed about all the bad choices she had made along the way. After Todd disappeared, she should have forgotten the whole thing and gone to work for an oil company. Come to think of it, she had done more or less the same thing with her job at SDI, a parasite that lived off the crumbs that big corporations spilled on the floor. Cheryl knew that she was a sellout too, like Annabelle, but without the glamor, the celebrity, and the five million dollars. And at the same time, she was the world's most useless activist—no one cared what she thought. At least Annabelle had inspired people, even if she was a hypocrite. As the week went on, Cheryl became numb to the depression and the anger grew stronger. She wanted to bring Annabelle down and make her pay. After a bowl of caramel chocolate swirl, she googled *How to Be a Whistleblower*. The results scared the bejesus out of her, especially a list of questions for whistleblowers:

Are you prepared to risk retaliation to report this misconduct?

Can any documents be traced back to you because they are uniquely marked or because only a few people have access to them?

If you remain anonymous, will that give the wrongdoers the opportunity to cover up the problem or will it promote change?

Are you sure you're right? Do you have enough evidence?

Will going public help you prove your case or make a difference?

If you're discovered, what will happen?

Do you need an ally?

She did what she knew best—she made a list. She wrote down ways to expose the conspiracy, who she could contact, and what might work. She considered sending an anonymous package with the documents to organizations who could do something about the scandal, like Congress, the news media, or environmental groups. The problem was that so many people from all those places were on the Project Common Sense spreadsheet. Others might also be on the take, even though they weren't in the spreadsheet. She could post the information on social media, which she barely used. She had accounts, but only a handful of followers. Would anybody notice?

She was stumped. She couldn't think of a path that would lead her from her kitchen table to actually stopping the conspiracy. Picking up on the last question from Google, *Do you need an ally?*, she wrote the names of people she knew who might be able to help her:

Jack? (No, for obvious reasons.)

Paul? (No, he's Jack's guy.)

Cousin Bob? (No, he won't touch politics with a ten-foot pole.)

Nate, the local C4 coordinator? (No, he'll inform headquarters and it will get to Annabelle.)

Jeremy? (Maybe, but does he ever leave his studio?)

Mary Ann? (Yes, trustworthy and wise.)

Amy? (YES, of course!)

After staring at her list, she finally responded to Amy's eighth or ninth text of the week (*Where the hell are you? Are you OK??*) to confirm their Saturday morning coffee date.

Over lattes, bagels, and fruit, Amy pumped Cheryl for gossip about the dealer meeting.

"I have to admit it was about the weirdest thing I've ever done," Cheryl said. Amy laughed uproariously at the story of Lance Meadows and the influencers. Then Cheryl described getting lost in the desert overnight with Jack, but left out the part about Vastiati, like he had demanded.

"I have to ask the obvious," Amy said, "Did he put a move on you out there?"

"NO! He talked my ear off about his weird philosophy of selling, but that was it. He's a world-class mansplainer."

When they left the café, Cheryl said "I have to show you something in private." Amy was intrigued as they walked to Cheryl's apartment. 'A love letter? A diamond ring? An autographed photo of Lance Meadows?" she joked.

"I wish. You're not going to like it."

After locking the door to her apartment and closing the blinds, Cheryl told her about the briefcase, then spread the Project Common Sense files on the kitchen table. She pointed to the entry for Annabelle Sinkovsky.

"What the fuck?" said Amy.

"Exactly what I thought."

"What are you going to do about it?"

"I have no idea."

"Who are you going to show this stuff to?"

"I have no idea."

"What about Mr. Big Shot Sales Guy? He's your buddy now."

"No way! He'd bury it and get me fired."

"You and I could take it to someone high up at C4."

"A couple small-time volunteers are going to tell them their leader is betraying the cause? Who's going to believe that?"

"I see the problem." They were both quiet for a few minutes. Amy kept reading the files. "Is there anyone you trust to give you good advice?"

"Besides you?"

"Besides me."

Mary Ann shook her head slowly as she looked through the documents Cheryl had given her. They were sitting in a deserted park on a chilly winter afternoon. Their phones were switched off and inside Cheryl's car. "Honey, they're going to chew you up and spit you out."

"But I can't let them get away with this!"

"You'll ruin your life for a short blip in the news cycle, your proverbial fifteen minutes of fame. Photocopied documents are the only evidence you have. The people taking bribes will deny everything, say it's all a forgery. To have even the slightest chance of success, you need something more."

"Like what?"

"I wish I knew."

"Should I talk to Jeremy?"

"Look, he would move mountains for you, but I don't see what he can do to help you with this."

FLUFF

JACK PRESSED VINCE FOR MORE INFORMATION about Lydecker's request for a meeting, but got nowhere. Had Lydecker found out about the twenty grand buried in the SDI invoice? Were they getting dumped for a competitor? Jack knew one thing for sure, it wasn't going to be a heartfelt thank you for a job well done.

Jack met Vince in his office on the thirty-fifth floor of Mega Motors' vast skyscraper in downtown Detroit. After Lydecker took over the company, rumors about this building started flying everywhere: They were converting it to condos, or making it a data center, and moving the headquarters to a smaller place in the suburbs—or even relocating to Texas. Nobody knew anything.

They rode an elevator to the top floor C-suite. Walking down the hall to Lydecker's office, Vince said, "Hold on to your hat."

Lydecker stood up and greeted Jack warmly. "I'm sorry we haven't had an opportunity to meet before," he said. "I've heard a lot about SDI—all good—and the dealer meeting was a big success."

"Thanks. Your company is our top priority. You always get our A-team, the most talented people we can find." Jack was waiting for the other shoe to drop.

"As much as we love everything you do for us," Lydecker said, "I did review your most recent invoice for the dealer meeting. As I suspected, you're nickel and diming us. I don't care about the details, but it doesn't inspire confidence."

Oh crap! Jack thought. Lydecker had the upper hand just seconds into the meeting.

"We want to continue working with SDI, but going forward, we have to look at some belt-tightening, a little nip and tuck. We're facing unusual challenges in the coming year that will require commitment of major resources."

Jack braced himself.

"My job is to increase our share price. That means I can only invest in projects that improve Mega's bottom line. I've been looking at numbers until I'm blue in the face, but I don't see a clear return on investment for the money we spend with SDI. Can you help me with that?"

"We always do a budget review to look for efficiencies we can apply to the next year's program."

"Cost savings are always important and I'm sure you'll pay more attention to the cost side after today. I'm more interested in the return side. How do your programs move the needle on sales? What metrics do you use? What are we getting for our money?"

"We do extensive surveys and focus groups to understand dealer needs. Our research department is world class, the best in the business."

"One of the first things I learned in this job is that dealers are always happy when we wine and dine them and give them free stuff. But would they sell any less if we didn't do all that? Would something else induce them to sell more? Those are the questions I need answers to."

"You can't sell cars without the dealers."

"And they won't be in business without us. I need to make decisions soon about next year's budget. If you want to work with us, I need a solid proposal from SDI in three weeks. Make the case why your program is a wise investment of our stockholders' money. Show me a line of sight between what you provide and dealer performance—hard numbers, not the usual fluff."

Jack winced behind his poker face. *This jerk thinks we're fluff?* He knew that the worst thing to do would be to walk out of the room with his tail between his legs. It was time to sell. "We'll put together a thorough proposal that will provide all the evidence you're asking for. We can bring you more value if I can let you know what Mega Motors data will help in our ROI calculations."

"Talk to Vince about that."

"May I copy you on my request, so you'll know which direction we're headed?"

Lydecker looked exasperated, but agreed. His assistant would give Jack his email address.

Vince and Jack walked out. "Are you trying to do an end run on me?" Vince asked.

"The first rule of selling is to call on the top guy. I'm doing what I have to do." Then Jack asked Vince for help with the proposal. "If Walter tells me to give you some information, I will, but then you're on your own. He also wants a proposal from me on a dealer program done completely in house."

Jack was furious. *I saved this guy's ass and now he's looking to knife me in the back.* But Jack had a bigger problem. Lydecker was clearly laying the groundwork to dump SDI. He was going to make Jack jump through hoops, then yank the business anyway. The fix was in. He was messing with Jack's meticulously planned retirement strategy. *I'll show that SOB!*

Regression

The faces around the table were glum and glummer when Jack told the team about the mess they were in. "He called it fluff, right to my face. This whole account is going up in smoke unless we can figure out something fucking good. I told Lydecker you were the A-team. Now's your chance to prove it."

Paul had brought in heavy hitters from around the company, in addition to his core team of himself, Cheryl, Mavis, and Rick. Cheryl chuckled inside when Doug Ellison walked in. Mary Ann's nickname for him, "Dougie," was etched in her brain. Cousin Bob arrived from Research, followed by a couple of vice presidents from parts of the company Cheryl had never heard of. She was by far the most junior person in the room.

Ellison was thrilled to be in a meeting called by Jack Weatherly. So he wasted no time before showing off. "This looks astoundingly easy to me. We have mountains of evidence to support the trophy value concept," Dougie said with a big grin. "It's an airtight case. All we have to do is package it for Mega. Slap their logo on it."

Jack rolled his eyes. "Trophy value won't cut it, Doug. That's exactly what Lydecker calls fluff. He doesn't care which rewards are better than others. He wants hard numbers. Does a dealer program make money for him? And why does he need us to run it?"

The room was silent. Paul said, "C'mon. We have less than three weeks to do this proposal. I know you all have ideas."

"We could propose a controlled experiment. A cash program to half the dealers and the rewards program to the other half."

Jack quickly shot that one down. "If cash works, what do they need us for? We mark up the goddamned merchandise, remember? Do you seriously think that Mr. M would want us to show Mega that it's a lousy deal?"

"No bad ideas in a brainstorm," one of the vice presidents piped up.

"Sure. Then you go tell Mr. M that the business he's made millions from is fluff. See you at the unemployment office," Jack said.

Jack sat there with his arms crossed and a frown on his face. He was watching these idiots flush his retirement package down the drain. Cheryl had never seen him this upset before. She opened her laptop and began typing as a few more suggestions were tossed out—like doing a quickie focus group of dealer salespeople, to interviewing dealers, to combing through the rewards data. Which rewards did the highest performing salespeople prefer? Are their sales more profitable than those of the low performers?

Cheryl spoke up. "Regression analysis may be a method to get the answers that Lydecker is looking for."

Jack perked up. "What's that?"

"It's a set of mathematical techniques for estimating the impact of different independent variables on a dependent variable. I've read about it in connection with climate change research to predict the impacts of various emissions reductions on carbon dioxide levels."

"We're not here to talk about goddamned global warming!" said one of the vice presidents.

"For Mega, the independent variables would be things like the sales incentive program, dealer promotions, and advertising. The dependent variable would be sales or profit."

Jack perked up. "That's the first idea I've heard that makes any sense. I like the sound of it. Kind of scientific."

"Can the Research department do that?" Paul asked.

"In principle, yes. But we don't have much experience with it," Bob admitted.

"What about you, Cheryl?"

"I've only read about regression analysis. Somebody in this company must know how to do it."

"Track them down, Ricard!" Jack said.

When the meeting ended, Cheryl found herself in charge of putting together a plan for the proposal. Cousin Bob shook her hand and offered to assemble a team with her. Dougie left in a huff.

Helping Mega Motors sell more cars was the last thing in the world Cheryl wanted to do. But now she was stuck.

And the clock kept ticking.

EARLY BIRD

"HAVE YOU BEEN HERE BEFORE?"

"No."

"The early bird special is fantastic. Not to be missed."

"No thanks. I'm not hungry right now."

"Suit yourself."

Cheryl was sitting in a booth at a pancake restaurant. Night after night, she had stared at her list of potential actions to stop Project Common Sense, but they all looked either doomed or risky, or both. In her desperation, a new name occurred to her—Victor, the disgruntled activist from her local C4 group. Though she barely knew him, she had seen he was impatient and eager to take the fight to the bad guys. Maybe that's what she needed—someone who wasn't afraid like she was. She wanted to sound him out, but thought it was best not to show him the documents until she felt sure she could trust him. To avoid the temptation, she left them at home.

As Victor enthusiastically went to work on his Salisbury steak, mashed potatoes, and peas special, Cheryl began cryptically. "I've heard rumors that some in the environmental movement are taking money under the table from big corporations."

"Doesn't surprise me. People are scum. Give them a little power and it goes right to their heads."

"How do we expose it, if it's true?"

"Who cares if it's true? Never hurts to keep the bastards on their toes and let 'em know we won't take their 'gradualism,' 'build a broad coalition' bullshit. The planet can't wait for that."

"I saw a document with names."

"Great! That'll make it easy to expose the traitors."

"One of the names was Annabelle."

Victor said nothing. His face was expressionless. After a long silence, he muttered, "It's fake."

"What?"

"The document you saw is fake. Has to be. Annabelle would never do anything like that."

"How can you be sure?"

"I've been in the shit-disturbing game for fifty years. I can spot a sellout a mile away. She's the only person in the movement who has any guts. She's the real deal."

"I thought you didn't like C4's coalition-building strategy."

"That comes from wimps like Nate! When the going gets tough, Annabelle does the right thing. You can count on that. And she's coming to town soon. Give her the documents and she'll get the word out and nail their asses."

"The people who showed me the documents wouldn't let me keep them."

"Doesn't make any difference. Annabelle needs to know about this." He took another bite of his Salisbury steak. "You're really missing the boat on this early bird deal."

Cheryl realized Victor wasn't going to be any help. He was the environmental version of Dougie—a true-believing fanatic, convinced of his own brilliance.

A few minutes after Cheryl left the restaurant, Victor posted on social media, *Traitors among us! I have it on good authority that some in the environmental movement are selling out. I'm not naming names, but it will all come to light soon.*

When she got home, Cheryl read this and was mortified. But the post quickly sank into oblivion. Victor only had a handful of followers, mostly other aging activists.

SECURE

AT HER KITCHEN TABLE THAT NIGHT, Cheryl crossed Victor's name off her list. She was angry at herself for even thinking this hothead might actually be a good ally. But at least she'd had the good sense not to tell Amy about her dumb idea to involve him. That would have compounded the embarrassment.

She felt like it was time to give up on this whole damned thing. No one was going to help her. She was on her fourth ultra-processed, supermarket oatmeal-raisin cookie when the phone rang. Amy's cheerful voice came through. "How's your day going, girl?"

"Terrible."

"What happened?"

"You don't want to know."

"Have you figured out how you're going to stick it to the bad guys?"

"Not yet."

"Well, I've been Googling my ass off and I came across someone who may be able to help you. He has a website and podcast and specializes in going after corrupt companies and politicians. He's brought a few down over the years. People pay attention to him." She said the name, Russ Bissell of SunlightPurifies.com, and Cheryl looked for it on the Project Common Sense spreadsheet.

"He's not on the list."

"Well, check him out. And you can thank me later."

Finally, a lead! Cheryl clicked on the website and started reading. Everything looked pretty good. SunlightPurifies.com had been in business for twenty years and now had a small staff of reporters. Reader subscriptions were its main source of funding. To keep his independence, Bissell avoided advertising money as much as he could. The focus was on exposing greed, hypocrisy, and corruption at the pinnacles of power. Their work had led to high-level resignations and indictments. She read the *Tips* page with great interest. Bissell wrote about their absolute commitment to protecting the confidentiality of sources, whenever possible. He invited people with information to message him on a certain secure, encrypted app. SunlightPurifies.com sounded like the kind of place Cheryl admired.

She went to the encrypted app and opened an account with a fake username—*moldwarrior.* She spent the next two hours composing her message to Bissell. She went over it word by word, again and again. She decided to describe the situation without naming names.

I have documentary evidence that a car company is systematically bribing environmental organizations, journalists, government officials, and others to block fuel efficiency standards, EV subsidies, and related regulations. This multimillion-dollar conspiracy will launch in the next few weeks. With quick action, there is still time to stop it.

She debated with herself about including some of the Project Common Sense documents in her message. She attached them, removed them, attached them again, then removed them again. She still didn't feel comfortable about what might happen if she sent them to a site she knew so little about. After several minutes staring at her message one last time, she worked up the nerve to click *Send*.

She went to bed exhausted. The package of cookies was empty.

When Cheryl awoke the next morning, she had a notification of a message on the encrypted app.

Hi, moldwarrior. My name is Jill. I'm a researcher at Sunlight Purifies and would like to talk briefly to learn more about your information. We can have a secure conversation on this app. I expect you will want to talk after your workday. Please give me a time when you will be available and I will call.

A smile bloomed across Cheryl's face. Someone was taking notice of her!

Expense Report

CHERYL STRUGGLED TO GO THROUGH THE MOTIONS at work the next morning. All she could think about was her call with Jill. But first, she had to deal with the new nightmare she had dumped into her own lap—developing an ROI proposal for Mega Motors. She spent the first few hours making calls and sending emails to people around the company Paul and Bob had suggested who might know something about regression analysis. It seemed like every person she contacted said that this wasn't what they did and pointed her to other names and departments who might be better able to help. She was figuring out that most people at SDI passed the buck when they were asked to do something unusual or potentially risky. The only people she could find who had any remotely relevant experience were junior analysts in the Finance Department. She emailed Cousin Bob to see if he could get them temporarily assigned to the project.

All morning, the *SDI YAH!* app in her earbud kept nagging her with reminders about expense reports. "Please submit the expense report for your trips to… Scottsdale and Detroit. These trips are client-related, so our clients want us to submit reimbursement requests as soon as possible. Let's not disappoint them with late, inaccurate, or insufficiently documented expense reports. That is not the SDI way."

Half an hour later, a new message popped into her earbud. "Your expense reports for…Scottsdale and Detroit …are past due. Please submit them now. Would you like to watch a tutorial on proper expense report procedures on *SDI KnowHow*? It will make this task easier so you can return to delighting our clients." She yanked the earbud out and tossed it into her desk drawer. She heard a knock on the wall of her cubicle and turned around. It was Paul, with a stern expression on his face. "We need to talk about your expense report, Cheryl."

"I'll do it today, I promise!" Obviously, SDI took expense reports very seriously.

"It's a cash flow issue, Cheryl. The sooner you finish it, the sooner we'll get reimbursed."

"I know. I know. My earbud won't shut up about it."

"Let me give you some tips that will make the report a lot easier to do"

"Okay," Cheryl sighed. Help from Paul sounded better than the tutorial from *SDI KnowHow*.

"I'll buy you lunch. We can talk it over then."

On the way to the cafeteria Paul continued to lecture her on the importance of the expense report. "One little mistake and Finance can reject the whole thing. They're nitpickers."

When they turned the corner to enter the cafeteria, music started to play *Happy Days Are Here Again*. A crowd of people were cheering and applauding. They were all looking at Cheryl. She saw the oompah band from Sprint for the Spoils. Her photo was plastered across the video walls of the cafeteria, with the caption, *Cheryl Ricard: Team Member of the Month*. Animated confetti sprinkled onto her video wall photos. Paul beamed and laughed. "Congratulations, Cheryl!" She froze and her face turned red. She wanted to turn and run away as fast as she could. But Paul had his hand on her shoulder and was guiding her firmly forward through the gauntlet of well-wishers. Ahead of her stood a white-haired man in a tailored suit and tie, in contrast to the business casual outfits everyone else was wearing. His arms were raised in welcome and he had a broad grin. It was Mr. M himself. He clasped her hand in both of his. Then he gestured for the band to stop and picked up a microphone. "Cheryl Ricard, today is your day! Our small way of saying thank you, for all you do for Success Dynamics and our clients. You have only been with us for a short while, but you are already making your mark." Mr. M read from an index card while an SDI video cameraman recorded everything.

"Cheryl stepped into the breach at the all-important Mega Motors dealer meeting when her manager, Paul Boland, couldn't attend because of a blessed event, the birth of his son, Paul Junior. Cheryl handled meeting details, kept the team on track, and put out a few fires with her quick thinking. Account manager Jack Weatherly, who nominated Cheryl for this honor, can't join us today because of an important client commitment. Like every one of us here, Jack knows that…." Mr. M paused and glanced toward the crowd. They knew what to say and they said it loudly in unison "Clients come first!" The group applauded again. Mr. M continued. "What does it mean to be Team Member of the Month, Cheryl? First of all, you can park in the coveted T-M-M parking space right outside the main entrance, for the next month. Also, you'll get a gift basket of delicious treats from the cafeteria. You can share them with your team. Or," he put his arm around her shoulder and pulled her in close and pretended to whisper in her ear, though with the microphone, everyone could hear, "you could eat them all yourself. You have my permission!" He laughed and the group applauded. "But wait, that's not all. At the end of the year, you'll join with all the other Team Member of the Month winners for your very own Sprint for the Spoils!" At that one, the band began to play again.

Mr. M pointed Cheryl to the video camera. She managed a weak smile. Mr. M raised her hand above her head in victory. Cheryl wanted to die or, if that wasn't possible, to crawl under a table and curl up in a fetal position. As the people cheered, Mr. M turned his microphone off and whispered his final words into Cheryl's ear. "Jack tells me you've done everything possible to help him with Mega Motors. Thank you. We badly need to renew that account. Remember, I've got my eyes on you. So don't fuck it up!"

Tough Questions

CHERYL WATCHED THE MINUTES TICK DOWN on her kitchen clock. Her phone was logged into the secure app. The agreed-upon time came and went with no call. As each minute passed, her mind raced faster and faster, from visions of triumphantly bringing Mega Motors and Annabelle down to despair that she was failing once again, this time at the most important task of her life. She felt excruciatingly helpless.

At nine minutes after the hour, the phone rang. "Hello, is this moldwarrior?"

"Yes."

"I apologize for being late, but my previous call ran long. I want to reassure you about the commitment of Sunshine Purifies to your confidentiality. We realize that you may be taking a risk by reaching out to us. This call is fully encrypted, end to end, and is not being recorded. Do you want to continue, moldwarrior?"

"Yes."

"Would you like me to call you moldwarrior or are you willing to share a name, even a first name?"

"My name is Cheryl."

"Thanks, Cheryl. Please tell me about the conspiracy you mentioned and the evidence you have."

Cheryl told the story of the briefcase given to her after the Mega Motors meeting and the disturbing documents inside. She had intended to keep using the anonymous "a car company" for now, but the name of Mega Motors slipped out. So, she stopped worrying about hiding the names of the conspirators. When Jill asked her who had received the bribes, she said Annabelle Sinkovsky received the largest amount. It was a relief to get that out in the open. Jill was briefly silent after hearing Annabelle's name, which made it seem she was surprised. Cheryl did manage to keep the name of SDI out of her story, though she assumed that Jill could figure it out if she tried.

Jill's follow-up questions focused on the documents. "Who gave you the briefcase? Can we contact them?"

"A technician. I don't know his name."

"So the documents you have are photocopies. Are you in possession of the originals?"

"No. I returned the briefcase to Mega Motors after I made the copies."

"Why?"

"My boss told me to."

"What information does he have about the documents"

"None. I didn't tell him I had opened the briefcase. It was locked, but I was able to unlock it."

"Do you know anything else that can corroborate the authenticity of the documents?"

"Only that Mega Motors was desperate to get the briefcase back. I had to personally deliver it to their headquarters."

"Do they know you opened it?"

"I doubt it. I was very careful when I put everything back,"

"We'll need to review your documents. Are you willing to send them to us?"

Cheryl took a deep breath. There was no point in backing out now. "Yes."

"If we proceed with this story, are you willing speak publicly? Using your full name?

"Yes."

"It could cost you your job."

"I know that."

"Okay. We look forward to seeing the documents. After our review, we'll get back with you to discuss next steps. It shouldn't take long."

"Thank you."

"Thank you, Cheryl, for having to courage to come forward."

As soon as Jill hung up, Cheryl photographed the documents with her phone, then sent a secure email with the photos attached. She was elated that something might really happen. Also surprised at herself for agreeing so quickly to be identified in public. It was what she had long feared, but she said yes without a second thought. The words Vera had whispered in her ear came back to her.

Voices

Jack had to put Mega Motors on the back burner for a long-scheduled golf outing at a prestigious country club with James Chieng, his Neighborly Insurance client. Chieng was a middling golfer who combined a half-decent short game with weak, erratic drives off the tee, so Jack only had to muff a few chip shots to let him win. Over drinks after they finished, Chieng was pumped up by his "best game of the year" and began dropping hints about the latest, hush-hush strategies from Neighborly leadership, as well as serving up some juicy company gossip. Jack didn't see James as the sharpest knife in the drawer—he had already heard most of this information from his other sources—but it always made sense to pay attention to him. He was, after all, Jack's main client contact. As James rattled on about the challenge of overcoming the agents' discomfort with online tools, the fuzzy image of the Pinwheel Galaxy filled Jack's mind. Chieng's voice faded out and Jack heard Vera. "Everything is in there, Jack, and we'll never know. All we see is the little smudge. And we look the same to them." This memory kept popping up at inopportune times. The thought that he might be nothing more than a tiny smudge made him shudder.

"Jack, what do you think?" Chieng's question shook him out of his reverie. "When can you get a proposal to me?"

Jack was flustered and said "I'll put my team right on it. You'll see something next week." He didn't know what the proposal was supposed to be about, so he had to steer Chieng around to describing again what he wanted. It turned out to be a project to connect Neighborly agents with a team of hand-picked social media influencers, and give performance incentives to both groups. The agents were intimidated by social media and most of them avoided it, Chieng's idea, which, uncharacteristically, was a pretty good one, was to get them to take the plunge by working with successful influencers.

Late that afternoon, Jack took a shower at his hotel before dinner with James at the fanciest restaurant in the area—the kind of treatment that James expected. As the warm water streamed over him, Jack kept thinking about the smudge and the question it raised. What if he was nothing more than an ant scurrying back and forth on a pile of dirt? Jack had never been troubled by self-doubt. It was a waste of time, the mark of a loser. Now he couldn't let it go.

He got dressed and had a little time before meeting James in the lobby. He opened his laptop to work on his new obsession—systematically searching satellite images of the Arizona desert. After the tour guide declared that there was absolutely, positively no way that a complex of buildings could be anywhere near where the off-road tour had gone, Jack decided to find it himself. The buildings, and especially the flagstone spiral, would have to show up on satellite photos. Computer work wasn't Jack's thing, but over the course of a few late nights he had taught himself to explore a tract of land using latitude and longitude coordinates. He didn't want to ask anyone for help—it would be too embarrassing to explain why he was doing this. The work was slow and he hadn't found anything yet.

The phone rang. An unknown number.

"Hello. Weatherly here."

"Jack, This is Glenn Patroclus. We worked on some projects together a while ago, when I was with SkyBridge."

It took a few seconds for Jack to process the name. He hadn't thought about this guy in three years.

Glenn Patroclus had been Jack's key client on a huge program with SkyBridge Communications. One of those guys who loved the high life too much and had a great fear of losing his perch on the ladder. The type of client who had made Jack rich. He played this guy for all he was worth, though he knew Patroclus would blow it sooner or later. Which he did.

To prop him up, Jack had fed him intelligence and gossip he picked up around the company. Taught him how to sell the projects to the top brass, while flattering him so he believed every one of Jack's ideas was actually his. Glenn was a sad sack, if ever there was one. But Jack never passed up an opportunity or advantage that came his way. No matter the consequences for anyone else. Other people were not his responsibility. One day, Patroclus was suddenly fired, without explanation, at a delicate moment, right before the renewal of the big program. Jack's cash cow was put in mortal danger. He wasted no time and was on a flight to SkyBridge headquarters that very afternoon. He huddled with all the people he knew who were connected with the program, including the woman who had been put in charge on an interim basis until the executives could decide what to do. The program could get axed or, at minimum, put out for competitive bids. Nobody said a word about Patroclus, only that he had "left the company." Jack knew not to ask questions about this awkward situation. Clearly, HR had decreed silence. Jack put his curiosity aside and worked night and day to save the account.

He had to make concessions that cut into the profit margin, but so be it. That was much better than being tossed out on his ass. He knew he could build relationships with the new clients and, over time, work the profit margin back up. The next few weeks were a nail biter, but Jack's efforts paid off. His success at pulling this account out of the fire after coming so close to losing everything was a major factor in his reputation as an SDI high flyer. Mr. M gave him an extra bonus that year and a promotion to Managing Director of Business Development. The title, which came with a nice bump in his base salary, didn't change what he did. Jack didn't manage anybody but himself—that wouldn't be his style. He had little patience for the other salespeople at SDI. If they did things his way, great. If they didn't listen to his advice, or couldn't hack the sales game, screw 'em. He was going to sell whether anybody else did or not. That was the only thing that mattered.

Jack took a deep breath as the memories rushed in.

"Good to hear from you, Glenn."

"I'm calling to apologize."

"For what?"

"I'm an alcoholic Jack. I was drinking a lot back in my days at SkyBridge and I did a lot of things I don't remember well. So I want to apologize if I ever hurt you or made you uncomfortable in any way."

"Of course you didn't, Glenn. Don't worry about it."

"I've been sober now for over a year—fourteen months and six days to be exact. I'm turning my life around. It's a never-ending process, but I'm committed to doing it."

"That's great, Glenn. Congratulations."

"Part of my recovery journey is making amends to people I hurt. You were a good friend, Jack. You did a lot to help me in my career, but I was drinking myself down the drain, so it didn't matter."

"I'm proud of the work we did together."

"I'm not proud of anything I did then. I thought I was a big shot and could get away with whatever I wanted."

"How are you doing now?"

"I live outside of Dallas, work at Wal-Mart, volunteer at a homeless shelter, and go to meetings every day. It's a good life. What about you?"

"Same as always. Still with SDI, selling projects, trying to do right by my clients."

"I'm happy for you, Jack."

Jack made the obligatory offer to stay in touch. Glenn accepted, though he knew that Jack didn't mean it. He repeated his apologies and said goodbye. Jack put down the phone, closed his laptop, and stared at the wall. Glenn's sad story hung like a pall of smoke over his head. It swirled and blended with the final words that Vera had whispered in his ear to send a shiver of dread through his shoulders.

Dead Ends

Cheryl drove past all the gas guzzlers in the huge parking lot right up to the building entrance, where her "coveted" Team Member of the Month parking space was waiting for her. When she pulled in, she saw that her name had been added to the sign marking the spot. She wasn't sure she wanted that attention, but the consolation was that the busybody who had complained about her bumper stickers would now have to walk past her Prius every day. Before she got out of her car, she checked her phone for a notification from Sunlight Purifies. There wasn't one, just the same as when she woke up this morning and when she got into the Prius for the drive to SDI.

During the long meeting with Cousin Bob and junior members of the SDI Finance Department she did her best to concentrate. But the message from Jill she longed for, the one that might stop Project Common Sense cold, never left her mind. As she listened to the Finance kids, all recently-minted MBAs, talk on and on, she wished she had never opened her mouth about regression analysis. They had learned all about this essential tool in business school and were thrilled to be working on their first project for an SDI client. One wrote equations on a whiteboard while the others did their best to explain them to Cheryl. It was all very technical and complicated, and she was lost with the first equation, which described regression with multiple independent variables:

$$Y = \beta_0 + \beta_1 X_1 + \beta_2 X_2 + \ldots + \beta_p X_p + \varepsilon$$

As the day dragged on, Cheryl discreetly checked her phone a few times each hour. Nothing. The challenge of the meeting became clear. Hard, quantitative data was required to model the variables that could affect sales performance. And SDI didn't have it. Cousin Bob took her aside at a break. He was apologetic. "I know you want to do your best for Weatherly, but this is a tall order. Though you might think we do studies like this all the time, we don't. They're very expensive and clients don't want to pay for them or give us the data that would be needed."

Doug Ellison sent over his "mountains of evidence," which turned out to be almost entirely qualitative and subjective—focus groups and surveys with broad questions like:

What did you like most about the program?

Which items in the catalog appealed to you?

Did you tell your friends and family about the rewards you earned?

How much did the incentive program contribute to your sales performance?

(On a scale of 1 to 5, with 1 being Not at All and 5 being Very Much)

Despite the lofty claims she had heard from him on her initial tour, this was pretty thin stuff. She could see why Lydecker called it "fluff." When Cheryl called Dougie to ask if more rigorous research was available, he said "This is what our clients want. They're happy with it." And hung up. The Finance kids told her it was way too vague for meaningful analysis. One of them called it "basically useless." They could develop a model for the impact of the SDI program on Mega Motors sales, but without real data to feed into it, both about the program and other variables, like advertising, promotions, and training, no model could demonstrate the program's ROI impact on sales. Cheryl didn't look forward to giving this bad news to Paul and Jack. Just then, she glanced at her phone and saw a notification from the encrypted app. "I think we're done here, thank you all so much for your time today. Please send me your final list of data to request from Mega, and I will pass it along to Jack right away."

She excused herself and hurried to the ladies' room next to the elevator. She entered a stall, locked the door, and opened the message on the app.

We regret to inform you that Sunshine Purifies cannot pursue your story at this time. The documents you shared with us may be forgeries. Technical analysis by our forensic experts was inconclusive and cannot rule out that possibility. We're not accusing you of deception, but the fact that they were given to you by an unknown person raises suspicion. In our work, we have come across many instances of people being duped by malicious misinformation. Russ personally looked at your documents and concurs with this decision.

Our reporting has impact because of our reputation for credibility and our thorough fact-checking standards. We receive many leads and tips like yours which, unfortunately, we cannot verify. If in the future you are able to provide additional evidence to support your story, please do not hesitate to contact us.

"It's true, goddammit! It's true! What do you want from me?" Cheryl shouted at the phone.

A voice from another stall asked, "Is everything alright?"

"Yes, yes. I'm sorry."

That evening, she ate a dinner of ranch-flavored tortilla chips with green salsa and crossed Sunshine Purifies off her list. She knew she should let Amy know what had happened, but she was too depressed to reach out. She was out of ideas and it felt like time to give up on this whole damned thing. No one was going to help her. She glanced at her refrigerator with the blank space where Annabelle's picture used to be. As she picked the last chip out of the bag, a new idea came to her—something she had vowed never to do. It meant violating a commitment to herself she had kept for ten years. But at this point, why not?

She looked up Todd on social media.

After he dumped her, she had done everything she could think of to remove all traces of him from her life. Photos were torn up and mementos and gifts were pitched into the trash. On social media, she had blocked, unfriended, unfollowed, and deleted him wherever she could. She would have strangled him too, if that had been an option on the drop-down menus. Now, as she stewed in anger at Annabelle and the rest of the environmental sellouts, curiosity about Todd bubbled up in her mind. He must still be out there somewhere with all the other creeps. Maybe he could help her.

His photos were all over Instagram. There were ski trips, barbecues, and beach holidays. Cheryl studied them meticulously for clues as to who in the groups of smiling young people might be Todd's girlfriend, but couldn't find anything definitive. Professionally, Todd had worked for several nonprofits and congressional offices, some of which were on the Project Common Sense spreadsheet. Then she got to Todd's current employer—C4! Somehow, his name had never popped up in the many fundraising emails and newsletters they had sent her over the years. Todd was a special assistant on the staff of none other than Annabelle Sinkovsky. There was a photo of the two of them together. *What the fuck! He coordinates her goddamned speaking schedule!* This discovery drove her even deeper into a pit of depression. It was game over.

Cheryl was at rock bottom, out of ideas about how to stop Project Common Sense.

A tempting, safe course entered her mind again, like it had every day since she opened the briefcase. Burn the papers and pretend that she had never seen them. Never learned about Annabelle's treachery. It would be so simple. Her life had actually been going pretty well. She was succeeding at SDI—even won a goddamned award! The back rent on her apartment was paid up. Amy made her laugh. Jeremy's music lifted her out of herself. She could have a life, a future—which was an unfamiliar feeling. Then the briefcase blew it all up. It meant more than losing the vehicle emission rules and EV subsidies, which would be just the latest blows to the climate on top of so many others. The real disaster was Annabelle's betrayal. How could Cheryl trust anybody ever again?

Even Jack's cheerful greed and half-baked philosophy of selling was beginning to look better to her. If everyone else was out for themselves, why shouldn't she do the same? Life would be a lot easier without the guilt about the environment and climate change—where Cheryl knew that whatever she did wouldn't be enough.

Jack was right when he said, "Your problem is nobody's buying what you're selling." So why not sell what people actually want to buy? Like competence, attention to detail, and problem-solving. There's always a market for them—

all skills she had plenty of. What was the point of defining herself by the things she struggled with—controlling her temper, managing her OCD, or trying to convince people of things they didn't want to hear? Why pick the hardest fight of all, doing something about climate change, then feeling bad when it keeps getting worse?

THE LIBRARY

CHERYL DRAGGED HERSELF OUT OF BED the next morning. She didn't want to go to work, but she couldn't face staying home and obsessing over her failures.

Just minutes after she sat down at her desk, Jack called. "I need to talk to you."

"What is it this time?" she barked at him.

"Calm down, Ricard."

"Why did you set me up for that stupid award? That was the most embarrassing thing I've ever been through."

"Relax. You deserved it. And I told you I would work it out so you could do a Sprint for the Spoils."

"I suppose you're calling about the regression analysis?"

"Something else. But you can also update me on that." Cheryl offered to come to his office. Instead, he invited her to dinner at his house. "It'll be better—no interruptions. And Julie wants to meet you. All the good stuff I've said about you has made her curious."

That evening, Cheryl followed his directions to a gated golf course community in a swanky West County suburb to find a sprawling mansion at the end of a cul-de-sac. A fountain with sculpted birds, empty in the winter cold, stood next to the front door. As she rang the doorbell, she wondered why he had invited her here. And the secret of the briefcase still weighed her down. She couldn't let go of her failure to come up with any plan that had even a remote chance of stopping Project Common Sense. She knew one thing for sure—telling Jack about it would make the disaster even worse.

Jack greeted her with a big smile and led her into a two-story entrance hall with a marble floor. Julie Weatherly, a middle-aged woman with a kind, friendly expression, introduced herself and ushered Cheryl into the living room, where they made small talk over drinks. Julie was the opposite of Jack—gentle, soft-spoken, and very interested in Cheryl, who found herself much more at ease than she expected. She worked up the courage to talk about her passion for fighting climate change and was pleasantly surprised that Julie listened attentively and made a few comments that she admired Cheryl's devotion to a worthy cause. Jack chimed in to say that he had given her advice on how to talk to people about climate change. "Like everything else, it takes selling!"

Julie announced that dinner was ready. On the way to the dining room, Jack reassured Cheryl. "Fear not, you're company, so we're going upscale. No Trader Joe's tonight!" The meal was simple, but satisfying—chicken breasts, rice, and broccoli.

After the dessert, pound cake with strawberries ("I confess this is from Trader Joe's," Julie joked), Jack excused himself and Cheryl so they could go over some business. They walked down a long hall, where he opened a door to reveal a library. Shelves reached up to the ceiling on three walls. Cheryl was surprised to see hundreds of books— history, fiction, essays, and biographies. Jack basked with self-satisfaction as he watched her astonishment. "Have you read all these?"

"A few." He pointed to a title, *Secrets of Closing the* Sale by Zig Ziglar. "This is my bible. It's saved my ass more than once." Another was a biography of Arnold Palmer "You can always learn from the greats." Then another about the wine regions of France "I don't give a damn about wine, but I don't want to sound like an idiot with wine snob clients."

"It's a beautiful library."

"When we built this house, I had my decorator get the books. I told her to make me look smart and cultured. She went to estate sales all over town. Everyone who comes in here has the same reaction as you. 'How could this be the same Jack who can sell iceboxes to Eskimos?' I love it!"

"Do you want an update on the proposal?"

"Sure."

"We can't develop a credible ROI model with SDI data. Ellison's research is useless. Bob agrees. The only way to make it work is to get real numbers from Mega: sales, advertising, and more."

"Tell me what you need and I'll ask Vince for it, but I wouldn't worry too much about it."

"What?" Cheryl was flabbergasted.

"I'm pretty certain Lydecker's going to fire us no matter what we do."

"Why?"

"Beats me. Maybe he believes his own bullshit about ROI. Or he knows something we don't know." Cheryl felt a shiver of guilt. *Is this about the briefcase? Does Lydecker know what I've done?*

"Could it just be his…uhm, common sense?"

"Huh?" Jack's confused look told Cheryl that he didn't know anything about Project Common Sense. That was a relief.

"Whatever it is, our Mega Motors account looks like it's going bye-bye. It would take a fucking miracle to save it. My retirement package is toast."

"We're giving it our best shot, Jack."

"I know you are, but I'm not expecting it to work. I can tell all this to you, Ricard, but don't breathe a word to the team. They couldn't handle it—especially Paul."

"You asked me here just to tell me that we're going to lose the account?"

"No, something much more important." He sat down behind his desk. Cheryl sat in front of it.

"Do I look crazy to you?"

She was puzzled.

"Because I'm beginning to wonder about myself. Do you remember the night with Vera, Tycho, and the other wackos?"

"Of course."

"And how that numbskull tour guide said there was no such place out there?"

"Yeah."

"He pissed me off big time, so I've been determined to prove him wrong." He swiveled the computer display around so Cheryl could see it. "I started searching photos on Google Earth. Have you heard of that?"

"Sure."

"I found a video online that showed me how to search by coordinates. So I did."

He pulled up a satellite photo of a piece of desert with a grid of latitude and longitude superimposed on it. "Turns out that Google Earth isn't very high resolution, but you can buy more detailed satellite photos. Now I can zoom in real close and move systematically, like I'm flying a fucking drone."

"Did someone help you with this?"

"No way! Do you think I want anybody to know what I'm doing?"

He tapped on his keyboard and rows of red X's appeared in all the squares of the grid. "I searched an area twenty miles on each side. It took a long time. There isn't a goddamned thing out there but rocks, sand, cactus, and scrub. But we saw those buildings, didn't we? And looked through the telescope?"

She nodded her head.

"I can't get my mind off those wackos. What were they doing out there?"

"I don't know."

"Do you still think about them?"

"Yeah, but I've had some other stuff on my mind."

"And Vera talked to us before we left. Do you remember?" She nodded again.

"When she whispered in my ear, she freaked me out."

"What did she say?"

"'Don't throw your life away.' The same thing she said to you."

"No. Mine was different."

"So she thought that *I'm* throwing *my* life away? What the fuck!"

Cheryl had thought Jack looked pretty down in the team meeting a few days ago, but this was worse. He stared at her intently. "Then what did she say to you?"

"Wishing for answers won't help you."

"What answers?"

"I don't know. I think she was telling me to take chances."

He shook his head. "What are we going to do with this, Ricard? Either we dreamed it all or we're stuck in some kind of weird shit."

They sat there in silence. Jack's mask of bravado was gone. Cheryl came close to saying something about the briefcase, but she didn't think he could handle it right now.

He looked confused and scared. And if she was going to follow through on her current plan to burn the papers and lead a normal life, there was no point in telling her secret.

At the front door, Julie insisted Cheryl take the leftover pound cake. "Jack will just pig out on it, which is the last thing he needs." On her drive home, Cheryl second-guessed herself about not telling Jack about the briefcase. He had opened up to her in a surprising way. Maybe she should have trusted him to see where it would lead.

Vera's right. I need to take more chances. The thought terrified her.

Circus Vastia

"You had dinner at his house?"

Amy was bowled over.

"We had some business to discuss. And his wife wanted to meet me."

Cheryl described the evening and the library of books Jack had never read, but left out the details about his search of satellite images.

"Did you say anything about the briefcase?"

"Hell no! He's the last person on earth who would help me. And by the way, Sunshine Purifies said they couldn't use the story."

"What?"

"They're worried the documents may be fake. So, I've run out of ideas about what to do. It's too late now. The announcement is happening in two weeks."

Amy hadn't seen Cheryl look this low since the day she got fired by the plumbing company.

"Hey, you're going to get past this. Don't be so hard on yourself. No one could have stopped them."

As they left their Saturday morning café, a flyer stapled to a telephone pole caught Cheryl's eye. She stopped to read it:

Are you a fool in love?
A fool seeking love?
Or just a fool (like most of us)?
Maybe you need …

An Evening of Jokes and Ideas

Circus Vastia

Tonight Only
8:00 PM
Odd Fellows Hall
3134 Wyoming
Free (as a bird)!

A shiver tingled up her spine.

"We're going to *that*!"

"Looks like another sketchy, low rent comedy show. Don't we have more important things to worry about?"

"It's right here in the neighborhood. We're going!" Cheryl insisted.

"Why?"

"Because of that night I spent in the desert."

"Was someone telling jokes?"

"Maybe."

She saw the confusion on Amy's face. "I'll fill you in later." Cheryl took out her phone, snapped a photo of the flyer, and started typing.

"What are you doing?"

"Texting Jack. He's got to see this."

"Mr. Super Salesman? Why?" Now Amy was thoroughly bewildered.

Time flew as Cheryl breezed through her afternoon cleaning routine. It had never gone so smoothly.

Cheryl and Amy waited on the sidewalk for Jack, their breath steaming in the cold winter evening. Other patrons, mostly urban hipsters and a few older people, passed them to enter the building through doors covered with Circus Vastia flyers. Jack rushed up to them a few minutes before eight. He apologized for being late—he had never been in this neighborhood before and had to hunt for a parking space. Cheryl introduced him and Amy to each other. Amy looked him over closely, this Superman from Bizarro World she had heard so much about. He didn't live up to her imagination—he looked like a basic, boring, middle-aged white guy, wearing a tan camel hair overcoat and tasseled loafers. He was one more odd thing about this show that Cheryl had dragged her to. He held open the door for Amy and Cheryl to lead the way inside.

They found places to sit and waited as people kept coming in. Cheryl was surprised there were so many. The small auditorium had seen better days. The walls were a pale, dingy tan and the two hundred or so seats were bare wood. Four musicians were setting up in the orchestra pit, in front of a stage with a closed curtain framed by a proscenium with Art Deco zigzag designs. Jack said to Cheryl, "Do you think?"

"We're about to find out."

The house lights dimmed and the curtain rose to reveal a dark, empty stage. A lone spotlight shined onto a wooden stool off to one side. From the orchestra pit, an accordion played a jaunty tune. A man on a unicycle rolled onto the stage. He was the Master of Ceremonies, or MC, of Circus Vastia. He wore a black swallowtail suit, studded with sequined stars and comets, and smiled a goofy grin as he looped in circles around the stage. The other musicians joined in to ramp up the happy melody.

The man gestured for the audience to clap in time to the music. He lifted his arms again and again, demanding louder applause. Cheryl's eyes opened wide. She poked Jack in the ribs. "Look! Look at his shirt!" Jack saw it and turned to her with a big smile. The black shirt had shiny silver writing across the chest: *On and On.*

The man on the unicycle played hide and seek with a spotlight that struggled to keep up with him. He darted in one direction, stopped and raised his arms to urge the audience to keep clapping. As soon as the spotlight found him, he pedaled away into the darkness. The pool of light moved back and forth to search for him. Then he zoomed out of the darkness from a different direction to laughter and cheers. He hopped off the unicycle and took a bow. He walked to the side of the stage and picked up a microphone that was on the stool. He looked out to the audience and signaled for the music to stop. He brought the microphone close to his mouth. "So, I asked my wife, 'honey, am I the only one you've ever been with?' She thought for a moment. 'Yes, you are, my dearest. All the others were nines and tens.'"

A drum set hit a rim shot, *Bada BING!*

"I went to a store to buy some camo pants, but I couldn't find any."

Bada BING!

"I can't believe I got fired at the calendar factory. All I did was take a day off."

Bada BING!

"Ahh, That one took you a moment. Kind of sneaks up on you. How about this? I was going to tell a time travel joke, but you didn't like it."

Bada BING!

"Jokes! Everybody loves them. You laugh even when they're bad. Which brings up an important question. What's the difference between a good joke and a bad joke? Hmm. I don't know the answer, if there is one. It's way above my pay grade. But since I'm not getting paid, everything is above my pay grade."

Bada BING!

"So what exactly is a joke? How is it different from a sentence or a phrase? Or a participle? Allow me to illustrate. When you say 'the rotation of the earth,' that's a noun phrase."

An image of the earth slowly spinning in the black void of space appeared above him.

"But when you say 'the rotation of the earth really makes my day,' that's a joke."

Bada BING!

"So a joke is one thing that flips into another when you look at it." He held up his hand and flipped it back and forth. "The queen taught me how to wave like this. Some people think she was a royal pain in the ass," he reached down to pat his butt and winced, "but I didn't find anything royal about it."

Bada BING!

"When you open your eyes, jokes are everywhere. Actually—I'll let you in on a little secret—the entire universe is a joke."

Three masked figures, covered head to toe in white, marched onto the stage in profile. They stopped. "Yes, ladies and gentlemen, everything is a joke. How do we know? Because there is a funny thing called light."

He stood at stiff attention and bellowed "Let there be LIGHT!" The musicians played a little flourish.

"What is this light that some god or another may or may not have proclaimed into existence? It's photons. Tiny particles that zoom through space into our eyes. Bip, bip,

bip, bip, bip." Tinkly percussion music played. The three figures in white held out their fluttering fingers.

"Yep, that's it! Particles of light flying toward us show us the universe. But wait, there's more! Light is also a wave, an undulating wave that washes over us and caresses us." Dreamy cello music played and the MC waved his arms in a swirling arabesque. The white-clad figures turned to face the other direction. This side of them, which the audience couldn't see before, was iridescent blue. They moved with the same undulating motion as the MC.

"Okay, let's stop joking around. What is light really? Particle? Or wave? Particle? Or wave? Particle? Or wave?" As he said these words over and over, the three figures flip-flopped in unison. Cheryl's eyes opened wide. She noticed Jack's knee pumping up and down with nervous excitement. She put her hand on it for a moment to quiet him.

The MC gestured for silence, like a conductor ending the music. "The truth, the indisputable scientific truth, is that light is *both* particle and wave—at the same time. And it all depends on us, how we look at it. If we do an experiment that looks for particles, particles are there. If we do an experiment that looks for waves, waves are there. Now, if that isn't a joke, I don't know what is. Okay, so what? Light is kind of flakey to begin with. It just zips around and bounces off everything. Let's get down to brass tacks, things we can touch and feel. Like chairs, rocks, baseballs, hot dogs, apple pie—and brass tacks. Our old friends—objects, stuff, matter."

The three figures paraded back and forth across the stage juggling rocks, baseballs, hot dogs, and pies.

"All this stuff that we wrestle with every day is made of atoms, little doohickeys that combine and break apart in endless combinations. We all know about atoms. They can be scary sometimes."

Video of an atomic bomb explosion.

"Everything is made of atoms. But what are they made of? You know. Tell me."

Voices from the audience shouted "Protons! Neutrons! Electrons!" The MC and the three figures gave thumbs up gestures and applause to each person who shouted.

"You got it. Atoms are made of these elementary particles. Along with their little friends, neutrinos, positrons, et cetera, et cetera. We'll set those guys aside for now. People have invented machines that can create beams of electrons and protons, these building blocks of all stuff, and point them at objects. Electron microscopes, PET scans, and more. You can learn a lot from them, like whether or not you have cancer."

Video of a person lying in a PET scan machine with animations of the device scanning their body.

"What happens when we point a beam of protons or electrons at something? Since they're particles, they should bounce around like tiny balls, solid stuff. Which makes sense, because everything solid is made from protons, electrons, and neutrons. So they have to behave like the particles they are. Right? And they do! Finally, something makes sense!"

In relief, the MC wiped his brow with a handkerchief. Then one of the white and blue-clad figures rushed over to him and whispered in his ear. He nodded as he listened.

"Uh hmm. You don't say. Really? They also act like waves? With interference patterns?" He looks up to the audience again. "I now have it on good authority that the building blocks of all matter are, just like light, both particles and waves, depending on how we choose to look. Particle, wave, particle, wave. Another huge joke. Everything, wherever we look, is a joke. We live inside a universe of jokes. ARE. YOU. CONFUSED. YET? I sure am! Maybe we need a little space so we can calm down. The joke universe—or should I call it the 'jokeiverse?'—is ready for that. It gives us space, more space than we know what to do with. And—I'll let you in on another little secret—more space than we can imagine."

Images appear on the screen above the stage. First, the earth, slowly rotating.

"Here's our little home, spinning away without a care in the world."

Two of the white figures marched to the center of the stage. One held a sign that said "M." The other held a sign that said "illion." The image of the rotating earth got smaller and smaller to become a tiny dot, with the large, glowing ball of the sun off to one side.

"Here's our earth from a million miles away—or a million kilometers, for those of you who are fans of the metric system. It doesn't make much difference. How about from a billion miles?"

The figure holding the M shuffled it with another sign that said B. On the screen, the earth and sun got smaller and smaller. The earth became invisible and the sun a tiny dot. Saturn and its rings appeared in the foreground.

"How about a trillion miles?"

The figure replaced the B with a sign that said TR. The image zoomed out. The sun disappeared into a field of stars.

"Now, we're lost in space. You can't see us any more. You've all heard of a light year, right? Well, a light year is about six trillion miles—or nine trillion kilometers for those of you keeping score with the metric system. That's a heckuva long way."

The image zoomed out again to show a wider field of stars. One was in the foreground.

"The closest star to us that's not our sun is Proxima Centauri, about 4.24 light years away. They named it 'Proxima' because it's so close, only twenty-five trillion miles. Isn't that sweet? I don't think we're likely to visit this very close neighbor any time soon, which is too bad. Maybe they're nice to strangers."

An image of the complete Milky Way appeared.

"Here's our galaxy, the good old Milky Way—also a very tasty candy bar. It's ninety thousand light years across with a couple hundred billion stars, give or take. That's us out near the edge. Wave, everybody! I don't want to be a Debbie Downer, but our Milky Way galaxy is not the only game in town. Far from it. The astronomers now tell us that there are as many as two trillion galaxies in the universe. If you're a fan of headaches, try wrapping your head around that!" He put his hands to his head and spun around in circles. Cheryl turned to Jack at the same moment he turned to her. They looked at each other and smiled. It was like the night in the desert. Amy was staring at the stage in amazement.

"Numbers, numbers, numbers. A million, a billion, a trillion. Too much to think about. So let's simplify. They're all just—illions. Illions are numbers that are so big, they make our heads spin. So we don't need to worry about the details. When someone like me starts going too far into the weeds, all you have to do is say 'illions.' Say it for me. Illions, illions, illions."

The figure holding the M, B, and TR signs tossed them into the air. The figure holding the Illion sign paraded around the stage holding it aloft as the audience chanted "Illions, Illions, Illions."

"The jokeiverse is bigger than we can imagine, illions of light years across with illions of galaxies. Or, as we like to say here at Circus Vastia, it's vaaast." He stretched his hands out. "And it's made of things that are vaaaastly small —protons, electrons, and neutrons." He presses thumb and forefinger together. "You have illions of atoms in each cell of your body."

"I could say the same thing about time. Illions of seconds, illions of years. Because space and time are the same thing in the jokeiverse. As our old friend, Mr. Einstein, said, you can't have one without the other. But I'm not going to go into that now, because I don't have the time!"

Bada BING!

"So here we are, stuck out in what can accurately be described as the middle of nowhere, for a very, very, very long time. Our little speck of dust, alone in the vastness. That brings up a bunch of questions we can't avoid. What do we do now? What makes sense? Does anything make sense? All of us at Circus Vastia have searched high and low for answers."

One of the figures staggered onto the stage under the weight of a huge leather-bound book. Its cover was embossed with the title *The Answer to Everything*. The others gathered around. They threw the book to the floor and pantomimed as music played and the MC spoke.

"We debated these questions, wrestled with them, and danced about them until the cows came home. By the way, have you ever had to deal with a herd of cows in your house? It has a few downsides—from the cows' backsides." He pinched his nose and grimaced.

Bada BING!

An image of cows staring at the audience appeared on the screen. The music stopped and the figures froze in place.

"The only answer to the big questions we could find, the only answer that makes any sense at all, is simple. Amazingly simple. Be kind."

The words appeared on the screen above the stage.

"Be kind—to yourself, to each other, and to all the illions of beings who share our tiny speck of a planet. If you're having the best day of your life, be kind. If you're having the worst day of your life, be kind. If people are showering you with love, be kind. If they're being mean to you, be kind. We're all stuck here, so we might as well make the experience a little nicer. You know, fluff up the pillows for each other."

A collage of images flashed on the screen: faces, crowds of people, forests, coral reefs, whales, microbes, birds, snakes, snails, etc., ending with the cows again.

"One thing is certain. No one is coming to save us on our tiny speck. We can beg, we can hope, we can pray all we want. But we're on our own. We have to do the best we can all by ourselves. Let that thought sink in."

The image of an hourglass appeared on the screen. The stream of sand trickled into the bottom chamber.

"We are only here for a short, short time. In a hundred years, everyone in this room will be dead." He did his queen wave to the audience, "It's been nice knowing ya! We will have gone on to something else, or maybe to nothing. Who knows? So how do you want to spend your time? Kindness is hard. We'll never get it completely right, though we can keep trying. If you practice kindness, and work on getting better at it, when your time is up, you'll be able to die without regret."

The final grains of sand fell into the bottom of the hourglass. The words "Be Kind" appeared again, along with "Die Without Regret." The MC smiled and held out his arms in a welcoming gesture. The three masked figures held their arms out in three pools of light.

The audience was quiet. People were taking it all in. One person started to clap, then another, then a third. The MC held up his hand to silence them.

"Thank you, but excuse me. Do you think we're done? You came here to be entertained and we've left you alone in the cold, dark jokeiverse. You deserve better than that. Now, it's time for popcorn!"

The musicians began an infectious tune. The three figures danced across the stage. They picked up baskets with paper bags of popcorn and began to fling them into the audience. More figures appeared in the aisles, who also tossed out bags of popcorn. The audience cheered.

The MC signaled for the music to come down to a low beat.

"The jokeiverse has another surprise in store for us. Everywhere out there in the illions of light years of space, something is going on in every moment, every tiny illionth of a second. Protons, electrons, neutrons, and quarks—which are even smaller—are popping into and out of existence. Everywhere, all the time. They're here, then gone, here, then gone. Huh? How do we know? From a little piece of science you may have heard of—quantum mechanics. Yes, quantum mechanics has shown this to be true. This constant popping in and out, like popcorn, is a dance across the entire universe. The popcorn dance."

The tempo of the music picked up and all the figures on the stage and in the aisles were dancing and throwing popcorn around. The audience members stood and danced. They put popcorn in their neighbors' mouths. Cheryl and Amy joined in. They saw Jack still sitting in his seat and pulled him to his feet. Amy grabbed his hands and encouraged him to dance. He started slowly and tentatively, then with the awkward abandon of a terrible dancer. Conga lines formed and the hall erupted into joyous mayhem.

After a little while, the MC once more signaled for quiet. The music got low.

"The very best part of the popcorn dance is that it also goes on inside each one of us, in our heads. Remember here, gone, here, gone, in, out, in, out? You weren't thinking of an elephant, but now you are. Every second, new thoughts, ideas, and sensations appear. Out of nowhere. They aren't here, then they are, again and again and again. This is the greatest miracle of our lives—popcorn mind. Most of the time, we don't notice it. We're busy washing the dishes, eating lunch, walking down the street, or holding hands. But popcorn mind is always there.

"Every now and then, our popcorn minds really get popping, when new stuff comes into our heads faster than usual, stronger than usual. You've felt it. Aren't those moments the most wonderful feelings imaginable? Every discovery, every invention, every beautiful creation humans have ever made begins in popcorn mind. You never know when it's going to happen for you, so be ready. You have popcorn mind within you and it will lead you to amazing places—maybe even to the stars!"

The dance music amped up and all the members of Circus Vastia on the stage and in the aisles began to sing:

"Pop, pop, popcorn mind.

Be, be, be, be kind

Be kind, popcorn mind."

The MC said his final words. "Circus Vastia thanks you for coming tonight. Whenever you can, go outside and look up at the illions of stars. You'll feel small, very small.

But you'll also know you belong to the vast universe. Be kind and dance inside your popcorn mind. On and on!" The musicians came out of the orchestra pit and played in the aisle. The room was rocking. Ecstasy reigned.

The MC jumped down from the stage and danced to the back of the hall, followed by the masked figures, musicians, and the audience. Everyone paraded out onto the street, dancing and singing. Strangers hugged each other. Cheryl floated on a cloud of euphoria as she watched the intricate, kaleidoscopic scene unfolding all around her. She spotted Jack, who was standing still with a dazed expression as the crowd streamed around him. She caught his attention and he looked at her and smiled, weakly. She waved for him to come over. Amy appeared between them and threw her arms around their shoulders to pull them in.

"That show was seriously badass!"

Cheryl laughed. "It definitely was."

"What did you think, Jack?" asked Amy.

"Good. Yeah … good."

Cheryl saw that he was not his usual self. Something was off. Just then, two of the blue and black-clad figures walked up to them and removed their masks. They were Tycho and Vera, from the night in the desert. "Good to see you, Cheryl. And you, too, Jack!" Their faces were sweaty and their hair matted.

Jack did a double take. "I've been going nuts looking for you!"

"Well, you found us."

"I mean your place in the desert. People who know the area laughed at me when I talked about it. I couldn't find it on any satellite photos."

"Vastiati isn't meant for everyone," Vera said.

"Why me then? What do you want from me?"

"What do *you* want from you, Jack? That's the question."

Vera turned to Cheryl with a smile. "How are you, my dear? Have you found your answers?"

Cheryl was flabbergasted. Did Vera see everything that was in her brain? "Uhm, not yet."

"Being alive means not knowing what will happen and taking the step anyway."

Vera turned to talk to another person. A voice called out their names. It was Amy, waving to beckon them to come to her. She was standing next to the MC. When they walked over, she introduced them. "These are my friends Cheryl and Jack. This is Lucretius." They shook hands and told him how much they liked the show. He was thin and small, the opposite of his commanding presence on stage. "I hope it helped," he said, speaking so softly that Cheryl could barely hear him. He looked completely exhausted, as if his performance had drained every ounce of his life force. Vera and Tycho joined them and Amy held up her phone. "Selfie time!" They squeezed close together and Amy snapped a photo of all six of them.

Vera and Tycho led Lucretius away to other people who were waiting for their turns to take selfies with him. "I'm famished," Amy said. "Let's go to the Vietnamese place. I need more than popcorn."

"Sounds good," Cheryl said. She looked around for Jack. He was gone.

At home that night, Cheryl basked in the shimmering memories of the Circus Vastia performance. *Particles and waves. Illions. Vastness of time and space. The jokeiverse. Cows.* She wished she could always remember every image she saw, every word Lucretius said, but she knew the details would fade. Would the intensity of this experience lead her anywhere?

She went into the kitchen to make a cup of tea. As the kettle heated, she had a sudden fear. *Vera and Lucretius didn't say when or where they're doing the show next. I have to see it again, but what if I can't find it?*

The kettle whistled. She filled her cup and watched the color seep from the tea bag into the hot water. She looked over at her refrigerator, a cheap model bought by a landlord, which had stood in this kitchen for decades. It was plastered with Cheryl's magnets, photos, and flyers, except for the blank space in the center of its dull, scratched door, where the magazine photo of Annabelle had been. She imagined that the blank space was growing and would soon suck the entire kitchen, and her, back into the crushing burden she couldn't escape. What should she do about Annabelle's betrayal and Project Common Sense? Circus Vastia had been a wonderful, glorious distraction, but she had to figure this out. Just like yesterday and the day before and the day before that, it was now or never. She forgot about the tea and ran through the same possibilities she had wrestled with over and over, ever since she opened the briefcase. She got out a pad of paper and started making lists and diagrams one last time. *If I write everything down, an answer has to come.*

Hours later, after covering pages and pages with notes and arrows, and with the untouched cup of tea now cold, Cheryl was wracked by guilt. No matter how many ways she rearranged the pieces of the puzzle, she couldn't get them to add up to anything that would make this curse go away. She had hit the wall again. Circus Vastia was magical, but it was out there in space, too far away to help her. In a spasm of frustration, she wadded up some of the papers and threw them into the corner. She buried her face in her hands. Shouts and laughter by tipsy drunks leaving the bar on the corner were the only sounds in her apartment.

Popcorn Mind

The wail of a siren shook Cheryl awake. As it grew louder and louder, red and blue lights bounced off the buildings across the street. She jerked her head up from the pile of papers where she had been dozing. The siren peaked as an ambulance rushed past in a desperate race. She rubbed her eyes and looked down at the scribbled lists and crumpled papers on the table. Seeing the debris that proved her failure made her nauseous. She put on a coat and went down the stairs and outside into the empty predawn street. A few feet from her front door, a homeless man slept under a ragged coat on a sheet of cardboard next to the shopping cart loaded with his life. His pocked and stubbled face gave hints of the smooth-cheeked baby he once was. She stepped around him and walked on. The night gathered up its mysteries as a brightening sky turned to tinges of yellow and pink. Another wanderer passed without eye contact, wrapped in his own world.

Cheryl had no destination. The lost hope of an answer mocked her worthlessness and laid bare the futility of her life. She found herself at an intersection, where she waited, bleary and blank, for the traffic light to turn green. Two cars idled beside her. Obedient, even though the cross street was empty. The light, controlled by a dumb timer, gave its blunt command to Cheryl and the drivers. *Stop on red; wait for green to go.* No one was itchy to break this rule.

She liked that.

The tired drivers watched the red light, with only a perfunctory glance at the pedestrian on the sidewalk. The signal changed and they motored off into the world to seek joy and do what they could to avoid pain, to live, and someday to die. This moment was the closest they would ever come to Cheryl Ricard.

She looked around and realized which corner she was standing on. Instead of crossing the street, she turned right. After a few blocks, she saw it down a side street—the Odd Fellows Hall.

The building was dark. Last night's posters were gone. The sidewalk was swept clean and the front door locked shut with a heavy chain. A *For Sale* sign was taped inside a window. No trace remained of the astounding performance that had happened there just a few hours before. She spotted a tiny sparkle in the gutter and picked it up. A sequined star.

She was startled by a voice behind her. "You found my star." She whirled around. It was Lucretius, wearing a dark coat with collar turned up. His uncombed hair was tousled. "Did you like the show?"

"Uhmm, yeah. Very much."

He smiled. "I never know how people will react."

"It was the most amazing thing I've ever seen."

"Thank you. You're Cheryl, right?" She was shocked that he knew her name. "Vera told me all about you and your friend."

"You made everything sound so simple. But life isn't simple for me."

"The universe is both complicated and simple at the same time. We just have to open our eyes and take it all in."

She felt a sob well up in her chest, then pushed it down.

He looked at her with gentle eyes. "What's hard for you?"

Cheryl took a deep breath. She had nothing left to lose. "I don't think I can do what you said. To be kind."

"Why not?"

"I have to stop some people who are wrecking the planet."

"Saving the lives of fellow beings on our little speck is an act of kindness."

"But these people won't like it."

"Will you hurt them?"

"No. Just cost them money."

He laughed. "They'll get over that. Money is mostly imaginary. It's just a tool, like a pencil or a paper clip. Far less valuable than the moments of our lives we still have in front of us. Teaching that lesson is also an act of kindness."

"I can't figure out what to do. No one will help me—at least no one who can make a difference. I wish it all would just go away."

"The answer you're looking for is already here."

"But I can't find it."

"All possibilities exist equally in a quantum state. A little nudge from you and they collapse from maybe to yes or no. Staring directly at a problem, digging and digging and digging, doesn't work. All you find is more dirt. But you have to do that before you're ready to see. Then, when you look away, a path opens. You didn't find it, you didn't create it, but now it's there for you. That's when you get the joke. Like the star in your hand. You came here, you weren't looking for it, but now you have it."

"But it's not a real star."

Lucretius laughed again. "What's the difference between a star and the image of a star? We could spend a lifetime exploring the ramifications of that question. If you find the answer, let me know. Love the questions, live inside them. Answers will come, but they are less important. The questions are the beauty."

He clasped her hand. "Cheryl, the jokeiverse is a cathedral made of questions."

He turned to pick up his unicycle leaning against the wall. Cheryl hadn't noticed it before.

"I absolutely have to see your show again. Once was not enough. Where will you go next?"

"I don't know. Wherever I'm most needed."

"Don't you want your star?"

"You keep it. There are illions more." He mounted the unicycle and rode away. "On and on."

"And on."

At the corner, Lucretius stopped and kept the unicycle balanced with little motions on the pedals. He caught Cheryl's eye and gave her a cheerful wave. Then he disappeared around the corner. In that moment, Cheryl Ricard suddenly entered popcorn mind.

MIRACLE

When she returned to her apartment, Cheryl felt ten feet tall and was humming and buzzing with excitement. She was released from the tyranny of sensible outcomes and could do anything without fear. She had a way forward. It might not work, but who cares? All our little lives will be lost in the vastness, one way or another. She texted Jack from her kitchen table. *I think I found that miracle you were looking for.*

He replied seconds later.

Where are you?

Home.

Address?

She gave it.

I'll be there in five minutes.

Cheryl panicked. Worlds were colliding. Jack Weatherly was coming to her apartment, her sanctuary? The place looked terrible, despite her hours of cleaning the day before. She raced around straightening the books on her bookshelf, hanging clothes in the closet, wiping her kitchen table with vinegar. She hadn't slept all night, so she didn't need to make the bed. She sat on the sofa and did some of Dr. Pettus' deep breathing.

A knock on the door. One last slow breath, then she opened. Jack walked in. He strode past her, then turned around.

"What the fuck, Ricard! What the actual fuck!"

She looked at him. He was wearing the same clothes as last night. His face was haggard and pale.

"Are you okay, Jack?"

"I didn't go home. Didn't sleep a wink. Wandered the streets around here. Goddamned lucky I wasn't mugged. Drank too much lousy coffee in some two-bit diner with a bunch of derelicts."

"I didn't sleep much either"

"I had a great time last night, but it makes no sense. What are they trying to do to me?"

"Who?"

"Vera and that little twerp on the unicycle."

"Lucretius."

"I get what they're saying. We're tiny and don't mean shit. Okay, that's cool. But then what?"

"They said to be kind."

"Yeah, well kindness isn't really my thing, as I'm sure you know by now. So, by about the fourth cup of coffee in that loser diner, it all came to me. If nothing we do makes any difference, we might as well do what feels good."

He peered into her eyes. "You know what I'm saying, Ricard?"

"Uhm, yeah. I think so."

"The problem is nothing feels all that good. An ice-cold G&T on the rocks? I've had about a thousand of those. A birdie on the eighteenth hole? The other guy got an eagle. Closing a deal when everybody told me I couldn't? That one's pretty good, but been there, done that. So good feelings don't mean shit either. It's a mess."

"He said it was all a joke."

"Well, ha ha."

Cheryl went into the kitchen and returned with two glasses of water. Jack took a long drink and drained his in one gulp.

"You texted me about a miracle. What is it?"

"We can get the Mega Motors contract renewed."

"Lydecker will never go for that."

"Yes, he will." Cheryl paused to work up her courage. "Something happened that I didn't share with you."

She told him the story of the briefcase and spread the documents out on the kitchen table.

"Why were you holding out on me, Ricard?"

"Because you would have taken the files and fired me."

"Hmm. You're right. I would have. Definitely."

Then she told him her plan for the miracle.

"I don't know, Ricard. It's pretty slick, but you're asking me to do a lot. We'll both be screwed if this doesn't work."

"Any worse than we are now?"

"Probably not. We can't let Lydecker get away with his little scheme."

"And it's two birds with one stone."

Jack closed his eyes. After a few long moments, he looked at Cheryl and said, "Okay. I don't have a better idea. So let's go for it." Cheryl beamed and they shook hands.

He stood up to leave and looked around at the apartment for the first time. "No offense, Ricard. But someone who works with me shouldn't be living in a dump like this."

Cheryl waited until nine before she called Mary Ann to explain her new plan. Mary Ann pondered, "That would have at least a theoretical chance of success. I'll help you, but only if I can stay behind the scenes. And we'll need Jeremy."

"I can patch him into this call."

"Not now! He gets real grouchy if anyone wakes him before noon on a weekend."

Cheryl said she would call him then. Then she texted Amy to meet her at the usual coffee place.

After they ordered, Cheryl said, "I have a confession to make. Something happened and Jack made me promise not to tell anyone."

"Since when am I 'anyone?'"

"It's about that night in the desert."

"So he *did* put a move on you. I knew it!"

"No. No. No. We weren't alone out there. We were rescued—by the Circus Vastia people. They took us to this crazy complex all covered with colored lights. It was miles from anywhere. Then it vanished."

"Vanished?"

"Yeah, poof, gone. Jack has been driving himself nuts searching for it on satellite photos."

Amy sat quietly for a while. Not something she usually did. Cheryl continued, "There's more. Early this morning, I went back to the Odd Fellows Hall."

"Why?"

"I wanted to see it again. There wasn't a trace that anything had happened. Then I found this in the gutter."

She took the sequin-covered star out of her pocket. Amy stared at it and smiled. "Wow!"

"And guess who showed up? Lucretius."

"You gotta be kidding!"

"We talked a little and, right then, I came up with a plan to deal with Annabelle."

"It's about time!"

At noon, Cheryl got both Mary Ann and Jeremy on a call.

"I haven't even had my first cup of coffee yet!" he complained. Mary Ann told him to be quiet and listen. Cheryl began to explain the situation and her idea. Jeremy cut her off before she got very far. "Save your breath. Whatever you need, count me in!"

Wobbly

"Let's try it again…Again…Again…Once more… Again."

"I need a break. My hand is getting tired."

"Watch me. This is how it's done."

Cheryl studied Jeremy's umpteenth demonstration. He made the move look so easy. Mary Ann stood there patiently while he practiced on her. This was the first time in months, maybe a year, that two visitors had been in Cheryl's apartment at the same time. This invasion of her refuge made her anxious, even though the visitors were her favorite people in the world and were there to help her. Jeremy had pushed her coffee table up against a wall to make enough space in her cramped living room for the three of them to stand and practice the move without bumping into anything. Every time Cheryl tried it, something went wrong. Either she got mixed up at the beginning or flubbed the ending. A couple of times, she dropped the device, which sent him up a wall.

"You've got to get to the point where it's automatic. You're only going to have one shot."

She tried again and made the same mistake as the previous six tries.

"Maybe monkey wrenching Project Common Sense isn't such a good idea." Jeremy had an anxious look on his face. Cheryl had never seen him worried about anything before.

"I'll be fine."

"I don't want you to get caught. That could be dangerous as hell."

"Annabelle's not going to make a fuss. She wouldn't want the publicity. The worst that can happen is that I get fired from SDI. I could care less about that."

Mary Ann tried to reassure him. "I saw what she did at the meeting in Scottsdale. She's one tough girl."

"Maybe *you're* the one who's afraid, Jeremy." Cheryl said to Jeremy.

"Me? No!" he protested. "Avoiding responsibility is my superpower."

"What about you, Mary Ann?"

"SDI won't figure out that I had anything to do with it. Jack promised me, as hard as that is to believe."

"Okay then. Let's keep practicing."

Cheryl got into position. She smiled to herself at the thought that Jeremy was concerned about her. He raised his hand and said "Go." Cheryl stepped over to Mary Ann and did the move perfectly. Jeremy pumped his fist in triumph, then told her to do it again. "You've got to develop the muscle memory so nothing will distract you." This next time was also perfect. Cheryl was elated. He told her to do one more, but before she could, the door to the apartment flew open and smacked into him from behind. He jumped out of the way as Amy breezed in.

"I scored big time!" She held up a garment bag and a shoebox. "I found you the perfect dress and awesome heels." She realized that she had interrupted them and said sheepishly, "My bad. I'll get out of the way." As she walked into the bedroom, she called out, "With this outfit and after I style your hair and give you a touch of blush, you'll be turning heads on the red carpet!"

Annabelle was scheduled to speak in an auditorium in the Central Library downtown, with a VIP reception before—$250 donation to C4 required. Mary Ann parked the car a block away, across a small park. Jeremy sat in the back seat and fiddled with his equipment. He made Cheryl say "testing" and wave her hand in front of the brooch on her dress, which contained the hidden body cam, about a dozen times. He was in his element playing undercover tech guy. After final words of encouragement from Mary Ann, Cheryl stepped out of the car. She was careful not to hit her "updo" hairstyle on the door and felt awkward walking in her high heels and elegant dress. She clutched her well-thumbed copy of *Illusions and Delusions*. She took deep breaths to keep her anxiety in check as she wobbled into the crowded lobby of the library. It was full of sophisticated liberal types, who had a very different style than the Mega Motors dealers, though some of them were just as wealthy. She looked around for people she knew. A few of the local C4 volunteers were there, but fortunately they didn't notice her. She saw Amy at the reception table next to the local C4 hothead, Victor, underneath a poster with the cover of Annabelle's new book, *Hard Truths: Confronting the Myths of Our Changing World*. Cheryl waved furiously to get Amy's attention. When she came over, Cheryl whispered, "Don't let Victor get anywhere near Annabelle! He'll start talking and never shut up." Amy said, "I'm on it, boss."

Cheryl took a few more slow breaths to calm down and get her bearings. She felt a tap on her shoulder and turned around. It was Todd. *Oh, no!* She figured he would be here, but didn't expect him to be standing in front of her in the first minute.

"Cheryl? Cheryl Ricard? Is that really you? So great to see you. It's been what, ten years?" He leaned in to give her a perfunctory kiss on the cheek. Cheryl was shocked. Her mind went blank in a moment of panic, then she thought, *the jokeiverse strikes again!* She recovered enough to act surprised to see him. "What…what are you doing here, Todd?"

"I work for Annabelle. I'm in charge of this tour. Would you like me to introduce you to her?" This was Cheryl's chance. In her earpiece, Jeremy said "Bingo!" She was flustered and could barely think as Todd led her across the room to Annabelle, who was talking to a small clump of well-wishers. In person, Annabelle was even more glamorous than on social media and TV—tall and slender with smooth skin, hair tumbling to her shoulders, a radiant smile, and a sheen of tastefully applied makeup.

"Ma'am, I'd like to introduce you to a good friend of mine from college, Cheryl Ricard." Annabelle shook hands with Cheryl. "It's a pleasure to meet you."

"I've been a volunteer with C4 for years."

"Thank you so much. We need all the volunteers we can get."

Amy appeared out of nowhere and tapped Todd on the shoulder.

"Are you Todd? There's a problem at the podium that needs your attention."

Todd quickly excused himself and followed Amy across the room. As she led him away, he turned back to Cheryl and said cheerfully, "We'll talk later."

Cheryl was alone with Annabelle. Thinking of Jeremy's words "muscle memory," she turned on charm that she never thought she had. "I've followed your work for years. You're one of my heroes. I devote most of my spare time to C4 because of you."

"Keep up the good work, people like you are the key to saving the planet—by changing one mind at a time." Cheryl asked her to sign her book. "Sorry, but I don't have the new one yet." As she opened it, Annabelle saw that pages were covered with notes and highlights. "It looks like you've read it very thoroughly," she remarked with a chuckle.

"Many times," Cheryl said. "I have a question about electric vehicles. Do you see them as an essential strategy to combat climate change?"

Annabelle hemmed and hawed and gave an evasive answer, couched in "before making final judgments, we want to follow the science to carefully understand the costs and benefits." This confirmed what Cheryl had seen in the briefcase—Annabelle was bought and paid for.

Then Cheryl asked if she could take a selfie. Annabelle smiled as Cheryl stood next to her and held up her phone. She pulled Annabelle close with her arm around her shoulder. After snapping the picture, Cheryl said. "I have one more question. What's your position on Project Common Sense?" Annabelle's eyes opened wide and the color drained out of her face. "Uhm, I have no idea what you're talking about."

"Sure you do. Project Common Sense. Mega Motors. They're paying you pretty well. Your price was what, five million bucks?" Annabelle abruptly turned around and elbowed through the crowd to get away. Cheryl shivered with adrenaline as Annabelle fled. In her earbud, she heard Jeremy's excited voice. "You nailed her! I heard and saw everything. The look on her face was priceless!"

"What about the bug?"

"The eagle has landed. All coming in loud and clear. Hope she doesn't find it for a while." Jeremy, through mysterious connections he didn't explain, had acquired a tiny microphone and transmitter ("weapons grade") that was about the size of a ladybug. "Cost me a pretty penny. My contribution to the cause." His insistence on making Cheryl practice planting the bug, adhesive side down, on Mary Ann's shoulder over and over had paid off.

Cheryl left the building as fast as she could. She caught a glimpse of Amy buttonholing the confused Todd by the podium. As she hurried past the reception table, Victor spotted her and waved. She ignored him and pushed her way through the revolving door onto the front steps of the library. She ran across the park to Mary Ann's car. After she got in, Mary Ann hugged her and Jeremy gave her the report.

"It only lasted a few minutes. Then either the battery crapped out or someone pulled the bug off. But we did pretty well. I picked up this conversation right after you left her." He played the audio:

> *Annabelle: We got a problem, a big fucking problem.*
> *Voice: [muffled]*
> *Annabelle: A random nobody just asked me about Project Common Sense. Someone's been leaking!*
> *Voice: [muffled]*
> *Annabelle: She knew the amount of my advance! This is a shitshow!*
> *Voice: [muffled]*

"Stop! What's she doing?" Cheryl asked.

"Talking on her phone."

"With who? I can't hear the other person. It's useless!"

Cheryl slumped in the back seat of the car. She felt deflated.

"Oh, ye of little faith. The voice you want is in there and I'll pull it out. The tools are in my bag of tricks at home.

Give me some time. This ain't thirty minutes or less pizza delivery."

"Jeremy knows what he's doing," Mary Ann said.

After Mary Ann dropped her off, Cheryl trudged up the stairs to her apartment. She dropped her newly-autographed copy of Annabelle's book onto the kitchen table, then went into the bedroom to take off the uncomfortable dress and change into pajamas. She washed the makeup off her face and combed out the updo hairstyle Amy had meticulously crafted. *Was this whole thing just another humongous waste of time?* She went into the kitchen, got a bag of potato chips off the counter and reached into the refrigerator for a tub of ranch dip. Then she hesitated and picked up an apple instead. As she took the first crunchy bite, she thought back over what had happened. After years of reading and listening, she had finally talked to Annabelle in person. As she replayed the moment in her head, it was hard to believe that it had really happened. She opened the dog-eared copy of *Illusions and Delusions* on the table. On the title page, Annabelle had written:

To Cheryl,

Keep fighting. The planet is counting on you.

Warmest regards,

Annabelle Sinkovsky

"You're damn right I'm going to keep fighting. Screw you, Annabelle!"

Jeremy called at seven-thirty the next morning. "Got coffee? I've been at this all night." He had parked his car on the street outside Cheryl's apartment. When he came in, he laid his laptop on the kitchen table, next to the book. "Coffee before magic. I like mine strong and black."

While Cheryl brewed a pot, he explained his strategy.

Before the event, he Googled to find images of Annabelle talking on her phone. She always held it up to her right ear, which is why he had coached Cheryl to plant the bug on her right shoulder, close to where the phone would be.

Cheryl set a cup of coffee in front of him. He took a long sip. "Not horrible, but we're going to move you up to a better class of beans." She gave him an impatient look. He was having fun teasing her. He took another sip, then slowly opened his laptop and tapped a key.

> *Annabelle: We got a problem, a big fucking problem.*
> *Voice: What?*
> *Annabelle: A random nobody just asked me about Project Common Sense. Someone's been leaking!*
> *Voice: Impossible! I've kept this to a very small circle.*

Cheryl recognized Lydecker's unmistakable voice. It was a little garbled, but clear enough.

> *Annabelle: She knew the amount of my advance! This is a shitshow!*
> *Lydecker: Calm down, Annabelle. Have you told anybody about our arrangement?*
> *Annabelle: Of course not. Do you think I'm an idiot?*
> *Lydecker: The leak did not come from my team. They are completely loyal.*
> *Annabelle: What are you going to do about this? My ass is on the line!*
> *Lydecker: We stick with the plan. Your random nobody made a lucky guess. They don't have any proof.*
> *Annabelle: I was ready to make the announcement next week, like we agreed. Now I'm not sure.*
> *Lydecker: Are you asking me to sweeten the pot?*
> *Annabelle: Thank you very much, Walter, but, no, more money*

won't fix this. If this comes out, my reputation, my career, my organization all go down the tubes.

Lydecker: A deal's a deal, Annabelle. If you back out now, you know I can make your life hell.

Annabelle: Don't go there! You better fucking figure this out, fast.

Cheryl grinned from ear to ear. She threw her arms around Jeremy. "You're brilliant!"

"Only the best for you."

She texted Jack with the good news.

Closing Technique

Jack's opening move was flattery. He knew not to overdo it—a little went a long way—but Lydecker was the type who got off on having his genius recognized. "I asked for this meeting to be just the two of us because we both know that you set the strategy for Mega Motors. Vince does a great job of executing that strategy, but it's yours." Lydecker smiled. The ego stroking was working. Jack thought a bit more might help the cause.

"Before we go through our proposal, Walter, I want to thank you for demanding excellence and rigor from SDI. You made me and my team stretch in ways that, frankly, we didn't want to do. Your challenge forced us to realize that the way we have been handling your business wasn't good enough. Mega deserves better. And today I'm going to show you the fruits of our efforts. And I know you will want to continue to work with SDI as a valued business partner—one who brings out the best in Mega Motors and your family of dealers."

Lydecker smiled. "I've always known that achieving excellence in business requires moving out of our comfort zone."

"I agree completely." Jack said. "The thing we are afraid of can become the most valuable element of the business when we are forced to look at it in a new light." He handed Lydecker a spiral-bound book with the logos of

Mega Motors and SDI and the title *Investment and Return* on the cover. "Let's go through this presentation step-by-step. Please don't look ahead."

He began with an overview of SDI's analysis method, "a multivariant regression model that considers a range of inputs, from dealer incentives and local market advertising to national brand advertising and rebate programs. We map the interrelationships between them to identify the most salient factors and assign values to quantify their contribution to Mega sales and margins." Jack moved from this silken web of generalities to the equations prepared by the kids from the Finance Department. As Jack expected, Lydecker perked up when he saw the equations. Jack explained them using the phrases the Finance kids, Cousin Bob, and Cheryl had coached him on. They had been worried he would get lost in the details, but he waved off their concerns with "I got this. Smoke and mirrors is my bread and butter."

Jack didn't stumble once and was even able to respond to a skeptical question with "We're fully prepared to adjust and refine the model based on more granular sales data you can provide. We envision this as an iterative process in cooperation with experts from Mega." Lydecker nodded. Jack was pleased. *Maybe this is actually going to work...*

He finished the presentation and waited. Lydecker read the pages with the equations again. "Thank you for the effort your team put into this. You've clarified the case for your program. Now I can see how you would calculate the return on my investment. But frankly, it would take a better than best case scenario for your program to yield results that would exceed what we can get from our other options."

That bastard! He's dead set on screwing me over. Lydecker's string of velvet words sent Jack a clear message—he had no intention of buying from SDI. Whatever misgivings Jack had about Cheryl's plan suddenly evaporated. It was time to close the sale using a method that didn't appear in Ziglar's book. Jack gave him a smaller spiral-bound booklet and said, "This appendix provides a lot of backup data. You're a numbers guy, Walter, so I know you'll want to read it before you make your decision."

Jack held up his phone and said, "Excuse me. I need to reply to this message while you're reading." Lydecker opened the booklet. The appendix was the Project Common Sense spreadsheet. The row with Annabelle's payment and the scrawled comment in Lydecker's handwriting was circled in red. Lydecker was about to protest when Jack tapped his phone. The conversation between Annabelle and Lydecker played on the speaker. He was livid. "You're finished in this business, Weatherly! Get the hell out of my office!"

"Hold on, Walter. You haven't heard the most important part of my presentation. All of this can become public—or not."

"Did Sinkovsky put you up to this?"

"No. I imagine both you and she want all this to disappear. However, there are people who would love to see these documents and your voice splattered all over the internet. Fortunately, Walter, you and I can prevent that."

Jack told him the deal. Renew the SDI dealer incentive program for three years and drop Mega's opposition to the proposed fuel efficiency regulations and EV subsidies.

Lydecker complained loudly. "You can have your goddamned contract, Weatherly, but don't tell me how to run my company!"

"Walter, I'm afraid it's a package. I'm just telling you what these other people need."

Lydecker kept grumbling and Jack waited patiently.

Silence was the best technique for closing this sale. The deal was almost too much for Lydecker to swallow, but a scandal could cost him his job. The boards of public companies didn't usually look kindly when millions of their dollars were being spent on naked bribery for all the world to see.

Lydecker's bravado slowly faded as he contemplated his future, and he agreed to the package deal. Jack reminded him of the importance of keeping his word. "The other people will be watching."

Lydecker signed the SDI contract renewing the program, slid it across the table, and snarled, "You and your little friends may have won this round, but don't think you've won the war. It may take a while, but we'll get what we want. Someday, the political winds will be blowing our way."

Jack's ambush was over. He walked out of Lydecker's office with the signed contract, which included a hefty penalty fee if Mega cancelled it early. He had just earned his exit package from SDI. Now he could start building the home on his property next to the golf course in Florida. Well inland, of course. *Let the other suckers take their chances living by the beach!*

Totally Done

Immediately after Jack called with the news about Lydecker's capitulation, Cheryl emailed Todd to request a meeting with Annabelle. "Tell her it's about Project Common Sense." A yes reply came within the hour. *Tomorrow. 2 pm.*

On the flight to Washington DC, Cheryl mulled over what to say. Project Common Sense had been stopped, but she was still so angry at Annabelle. She rehearsed different approaches in her head, but feared they would all fly out the window once she was in Annabelle's presence. Would she be intimidated and tongue-tied, or lash out like she had with her brother and the plumbing company? Either would be bad. Would the courage of her popcorn mind abandon her?

Cheryl's anxiety sloshed inside her as she rode the elevator up to the C4 offices. When the elevator door opened, Todd was standing right there. He lit up with a smile, then leaned in to give her a hug. "Cheryl!. It's amazing to see you again so soon. I'm sorry we didn't get a chance to talk after the St. Louis event."

"I had to leave quickly."

He led her through the C4 headquarters, a maze of cubicles where young people worked at computers. "You've made a huge impression on Annabelle."

"What kind of impression?"

"When I showed her your email yesterday, she wanted to see you as soon as possible. I canceled three appointments to free up her time today. She only does that for very special people. She usually hates last-minute changes to her schedule. I hope you're here about a job. It would be fantastic to be working with you again! You were the smartest person I knew in college, and it was obvious that you would go far."

As they entered a long corridor, he gushed about all the fun they had in the old days—the hikes, the protest marches, their favorite pizza place, and watching the Al Gore movie. It only took a minute before Cheryl was pissed off by his cheerful chumminess, like they were still best friends. She stopped and looked him straight in the eye.

"Todd, shut up."

He was taken aback. They walked in silence to a door with *Annabelle Sinkovsky* on the nameplate. He opened it for her.

Annabelle's office was huge, the size of the obscene hotel room in Scottsdale. Windows showed a sweeping view of the Washington skyline beneath a cloud-flecked blue sky, with the dome of the Capitol in the distance. The surface of Annabelle's large, polished desk was empty, except for a closed laptop and a brushed-nickel elbow lamp—just the way Cheryl would have organized it. Was Annabelle a kindred spirit, who understood the calm that only simplicity and neatness could bring? Giant photo prints of nature scenes covered the walls: a lush, shady forest, waves crashing on a rocky shore, a snow-capped mountain, and the piercing gaze of a Great Horned Owl, whose merciless yellow and black eyes challenged all who entered, *What are you doing to save ME?* This was Annabelle's world. Cheryl felt a familiar flicker of doubt. *Do I deserve to be here?*

Annabelle walked out from behind her desk and shook Cheryl's hand. "Thank you for coming." She gestured for her to sit at an elegant conference table and offered her coffee, tea, or water. Cheryl declined. Todd also sat down, ready to take notes. Cheryl had absolutely no desire to have him here. She looked at him coldly, then turned to Annabelle. "Just you and me." Annabelle nodded for him to leave. He was annoyed as he stood up and closed the door behind him.

Wasting no time on chitchat, Annabelle asked, "What do you want from me?"

With that question, Cheryl's anxiety lifted. The moment had arrived, and she knew she was ready. She opened her satchel and slid a paper across the table—the Project Common Sense spreadsheet. Annabelle looked at the row circled in red with her name, the five million-dollar payment, and the handwritten comment, *The big fish!* Annabelle frowned and her brow furrowed slightly.

Cheryl sat quietly, then asked, "Why did you do it?"

Annabelle closed her eyes for a moment.

"Let me tell you something about power, something I've learned the hard way. Our side has a fair amount of power, more than we did ten years ago. But the other side has much, much more, and always will. Nothing you or I can do will ever change that. It was obvious that the fuel efficiency regulations and EV subsidies weren't going to survive. No matter what I did, the big money was going to win. I wanted to at least have some positive influence on the outcome. It's too late to prevent climate change. It's already here. I'm sure you know that. Another century of rising temperatures, melting ice caps, and global calamities is inevitable from the emissions that have already happened. However, I don't see the benefit of sending that message out to the world. People need hope or they'll stop fighting."

"You stopped fighting."

"No, I didn't. I got real. I saw how many people Lydecker was recruiting. I wouldn't have any influence If I were the last one standing outside the tent. Better to be inside where I might be able to make it less bad."

"Less bad? Is that all you've got?"

"You're naïve. It was strategy. If I weren't on the inside, they would do worse."

"Was taking five million bucks part of your inside strategy?"

"When they pay me, they see my input as more valuable."

"Or they own you!" Cheryl fumed at the self-serving hypocrisy. "You're the one person I counted on, more than anyone else. I read your books, watched your TED talks about a zillion times, and listened to your podcasts every Saturday. I volunteered with C4, knocked on doors, sat at a booth at the farmers market and got ignored by people walking by. I thought I was doing the right thing. I worked dead-end jobs because I didn't want to sell out. I was trying to live up to your example of resisting the forces of the monster corporations.

"One Thanksgiving, I got into an ugly shouting match with my brother—my big brother who used to whirl me around the back yard and tell me knock-knock jokes—over his huge, climate catastrophe pickup truck. It ruined the holiday for the family, and he's avoided me ever since. I did it to be like you, to speak the disturbing truth, to stand up for the coral reefs and the pollinators who are going to die because of us. I did it because I believed that you would never sell out, that you were better than the chickenshit politicians who will parrot any stupid, ridiculous thing a big donor tells them. I thought you had more integrity than them—but you don't. The only difference is that your act is slicker. I idolized you for so many years, and now I hate you."

"I'm sorry you've had some tough times. But don't blame me. I didn't make you do a damn thing."

"I'm a 'random nobody,'" Cheryl made air quotes, "and I stopped Project Common Sense. You could have done more."

"It's not stopped."

"Yes, it is. You'll find out soon enough."

"Maybe or maybe not. Lydecker doesn't give up easy. I made the choice I thought was best for the planet and I'd do it again."

"Okay, what if we only got half a loaf? You once said that a climate warrior should accept a compromise and keep on fighting."

Annabelle gave Cheryl an icy look. "So, what do you want from me?"

"You could start by giving the five million dollars away—to someone who isn't on Lydecker's list."

"What good would that do?"

"They might use it for something worthwhile."

"You've got a lot of goddamned nerve coming in here to lecture me!"

Cheryl just sat there. She thought that finally getting out her anger at Annabelle would be cathartic, but it didn't feel as good as she hoped. She took a long, slow breath.

"You're a lot smaller than you think you are."

"Don't insult me!"

"We're *all* a lot smaller than we think we are. It's actually wonderful. Because when we realize that, there's nothing in the way of doing the right thing—being kind to each other and to our tiny planet."

"Get the hell out of my office!"

Cheryl took her phone out of her satchel and laid it on the table. "Before I go, here's something I think you'll want to hear." She played the audio of Annabelle's phone call with Lydecker. Annabelle listened and cringed. About halfway through, she said, "Stop! I get it. You're blackmailing me. I guess you want to be paid off."

"No, I'm just giving you a heads up. Do whatever you want with this information. It's your life."

Annabelle stood up. The photo of the owl was right behind her. Cheryl looked into its unblinking eyes and hoped for its gratitude, but owls don't do gratitude. Cheryl reached out to shake hands. Annabelle didn't respond. She turned her back to face the window.

Annabelle now looked weak and pathetic. A weight lifted off Cheryl's shoulders—she was done, so totally done, with hero worship.

Exit

Cheryl pulled her Prius into the Team Member of the Month parking space. Her month was over, but she wanted them to see it in the coveted location one more time, especially now that her newest message was plastered to the back window—a large white sticker strategically covering up a C4 sticker. The new one read *Illegitimi non carborundum.*

She liked the idea that SDI people would have to look up the translation from Latin. A good message for the current winner of Team Member of the Month. Maybe it would give them perspective on their annoyance at losing a few hours of their precious month of better parking. Cheryl entered the building and told the receptionist she had an appointment with Heather Holmes.

"We're sorry to see you go, Cheryl. I remember your orientation, just a short while ago. This is a first for me. I've never done an exit so soon after an intake, unless there was a performance problem," Heather looked down at Cheryl's papers on the table. "Definitely not the case for you. First, you won Team Member of the Month. Now you're getting quite a generous bonus. My vice-president was reluctant to approve it, but Mr. Weatherly insisted. I have to ask you to sign a nondisclosure agreement about the bonus. If it became known around the company, it could set a bad precedent. Between you and me, it's very impressive."

"I did my best," Cheryl said as she signed. "Maybe you'll get one like this someday."

"I wish. The look on my husband's face would be priceless. We'll deposit the money into your bank account today. There's also a small matter of an outstanding expense report, but we're waiving that at Mr. Weatherly's request." Cheryl turned in her company laptop, phone, and earbud. She was glad to be rid of them, especially the earbud.

"We do a standard exit interview with everyone who leaves the company. There are a few questions I have to go through with you."

"Can we make it quick? I have a long drive in front of me."

"On a scale of one to ten, how would you rate your experience working at SDI?"

Cheryl sighed. "I don't know how to answer that. There was both good and bad."

"Should I put you down for a five?"

"Make it a six." Cheryl felt generous.

"What did you like best about SDI?"

"The people. Some are very smart and talented."

"Do you mean the creatives who work in production?"

"Yes. And others."

"What did you like least about working here?"

"This just isn't the place for me."

"Was the work too demanding or the hours too long?"

"No. I like hard work. I don't think I fit well into what you do here."

"What improvements can SDI make to better attract and retain people like you?"

"You're better off without people like me."

Heather had never heard that answer before. "Why are you leaving?"

"I have a better opportunity."

"Another company? Can you elaborate?"

"You wouldn't understand."

At the end, they stood to shake hands.

"You've been a real asset to SDI. You'll be missed."

"Not for long, I bet."

"Any final thoughts?"

"Yes, one for you, Heather." Cheryl looked her in the eye. "Don't throw your life away."

Cheryl drove across the country. Jeremy had loaded a playlist of his favorite music onto her phone, so the miles flew by. On the second day, she switched to the radio and heard a news report that made her smile.

In a stunning about-face, Mega Motors announced its support today for the legislation in Congress to strengthen fuel efficiency standards and offer subsidies for electric vehicles. "We accept these proposals as a viable step forward for the automobile industry and American consumers," said Mega Motors CEO Walter Lydecker. "The entire Mega Motors family believes that the future is now."

In other news, Annabelle Sinkovsky, founder and president of the influential Climate Crisis Coordinating Committee, is stepping down from her position, effective immediately. Her sudden, unexpected resignation is causing an uproar in the environmental movement.

On the outskirts of Scottsdale, she left her Prius at a used car lot, which offered long-term parking. She had no idea how long she would be gone, so she paid for a month. The deal included a driver to take her to her destination.

An hour later, they passed the gas station where she and Jack had been picked up by the helicopter. After a few more miles, Cheryl told the driver to pull over.

"Why? There's nothing here. Are you sure you'll be okay?"

She lifted her backpack out of the back seat. "I'm going for a hike, then doing some camping."

After the car drove away, she hoisted the backpack onto her shoulders and adjusted the straps. She took her phone out of her pocket. The lock screen showed the photo of herself, Jack, and Amy with Vera, Tycho, and Lucretius—a good omen, she hoped. There was still a weak phone signal here, so she snapped a selfie and sent it to Jack with a short text: *I'll be looking at the stars tonight. Hope you will too.*

He surprised her with a quick reply: a photo of a waterlogged golf course. *I'll try, but it's been raining cats and dogs for days down here. Even the alligators are sick of it. Though it's hard to tell with an alligator.*

She sent her selfie to Amy: *Are you making good use of your present from Miltina?*

Then to Mary Ann: *Thanks for everything. I'll be there to see you in Streetcar.*

She typed one more text—to Jeremy: *The playlist is awesome!! I listened to it three times. I have so many questions. I can't wait to see you again, but you know I have to do this important thing first.*

She was about to add one more line, then hesitated. A moment of doubt trembled inside her.

Maybe I shouldn't say this. Is it too much?

Then she remembered what Vera had said to her. She took a deep breath, then typed: *kisses, c*

She quickly pressed *Send* before she could change her mind.

Then she turned off the phone and hoisted the pack onto her shoulders. The sequined star sewn onto its back sparkled as she walked into the scrub. She looked around until she found what could be the trail that she and Jack had come down in the dune buggy a few months before. It was hard to be sure, but she started up it. One way or the other, she would get to the place she was looking for. Either she would find it or it would find her.

Tonight, millions of stars were waiting for Cheryl Ricard.

The End

Acknowledgements

Very special thanks to the late Ollie Richards and to Joe Hasemueller. Their stories and humor helped bring SDI to life.

Thanks to all the wonderful people who read drafts and offered suggestions that made this book better:

Jerry Adler
Kim Block
Mario Borunda
Andrea Bruce
Charlie Claggett
Joe Hasemueller
Bradley King
Mark Tucker
Sarah von Pollaro
Camille von Schrader
Patty Wirth

About the Author

Eric von Schrader was born and raised in St. Louis, Missouri, where his books are set. His *Intersecting Worlds* trilogy grew out of thoughts about what the city is, what it was (all the way back to ancient times), and what it might become.

Writing is the best adventure he's discovered. He enjoys dreaming, speculating, and crafting stories that take readers on surprising journeys.

Before writing fiction, he made documentary films, produced television shows, helped start a community radio station, and worked as a writer and consultant for businesses.

He and his wife live near the ocean in Carpinteria, California.

Eric loves hearing from readers. Visit his website at ericvonschrader.com where you can send a message and join his mailing list.

Follow him on Facebook at facebook.com/auniverselesstraveled .

www.ingramcontent.com/pod-product-compliance
Lightning Source LLC
Chambersburg PA
CBHW020322180726
47991CB00018B/222